KING ARTHUR
AND THE KNIGHTS
OF THE ROUND TABLE

by M. C. Hall

illustrated by C. E. Richards

LIBRARIAN REVIEWER
Allyson A.W. Lyga MS - Library Media/Graphic Novel Consultant
Fulbright Memorial Fund Scholar, author

READING CONSULTANT
Mark DeYoung - Classroom Teacher, Edina Public Schools, Minnesota
BA in Elementary Education, Central College
MS in Curriculum & Instruction, University of Minnesota

23.93

Graphic Revolve is published by Stone Arch Books,
151 Good Counsel Drive, P.O. Box 669,
Mankato, Minnesota 56002.
www.stonearchbooks.com

Library of Congress Cataloging-in-Publication Data
Hall, Margaret, 1947–
    King Arthur and the Knights of the Round Table/ retold by M. C. Hall; illustrated
by C. E. Richards.
    p. cm.—(Graphic Revolve)
    ISBN-13: 978-1-59889-048-8 (hardcover)
    ISBN-10: 1-59889-048-4 (hardcover)
    ISBN-13: 978-1-59889-218-5 (paperback)
    ISBN-10: 1-59889-218-5 (paperback)
    1. Graphic novels. I. Richards, C. E. II. Title. III. Series.
PN6727.H255K56 2007
741.5'973—dc22   2006007693

Summary: In a world of wizards, giants, and dragons, King Arthur and the Knights of the
Round Table are the only defense against the forces of evil that threaten the kingdom of
Camelot.

Credits
Art Director: Heather Kindseth
Cover Graphic Designer: Heather Kindseth and Kay Fraser
Interior Graphic Designer: Heather Kindseth

1 2 3 4 5 6 11 10 09 08 07 06

Printed in the United States of America.

TABLE OF CONTENTS

INTRODUCING . . .

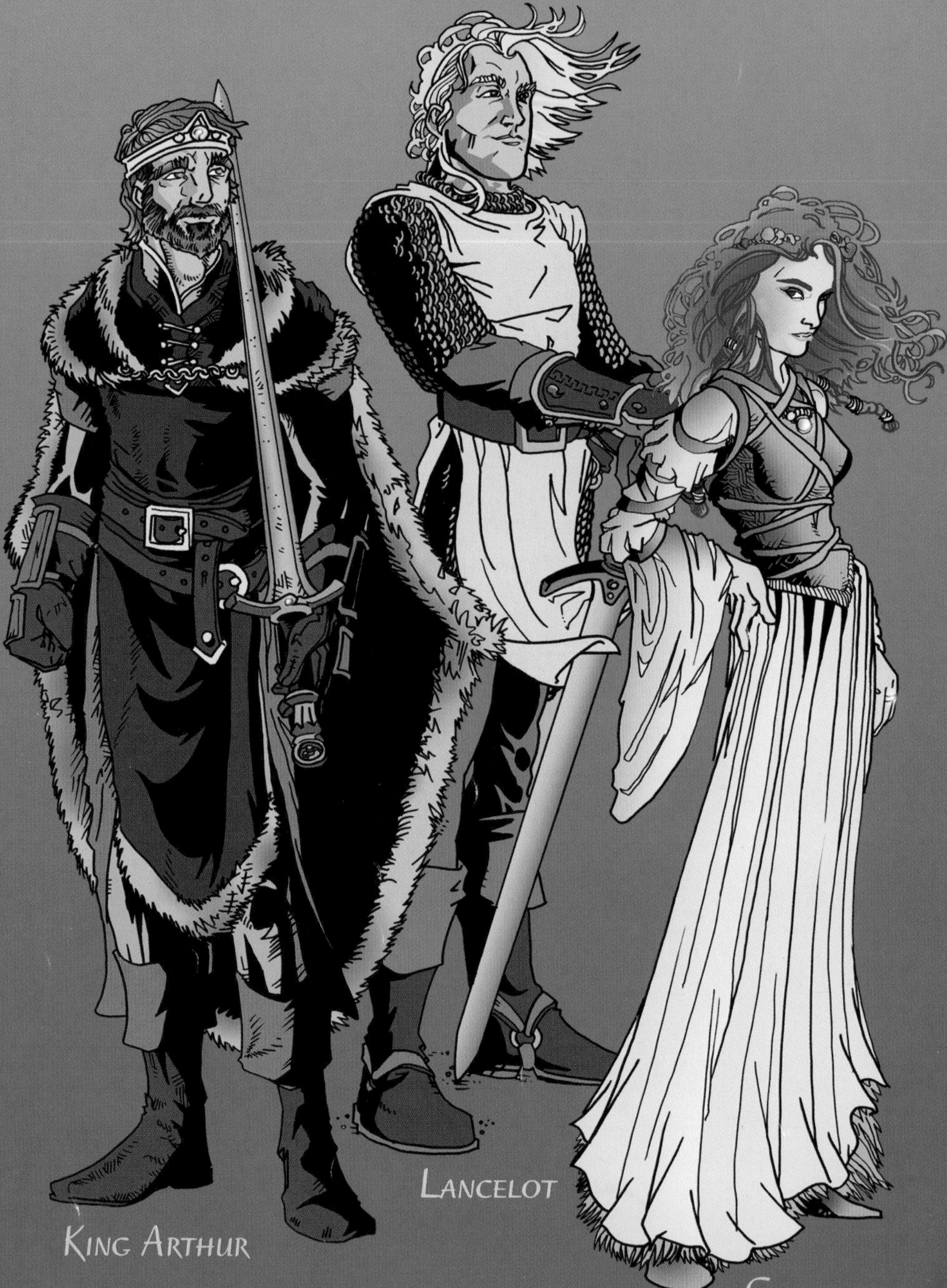

Lancelot
King Arthur
Guinevere

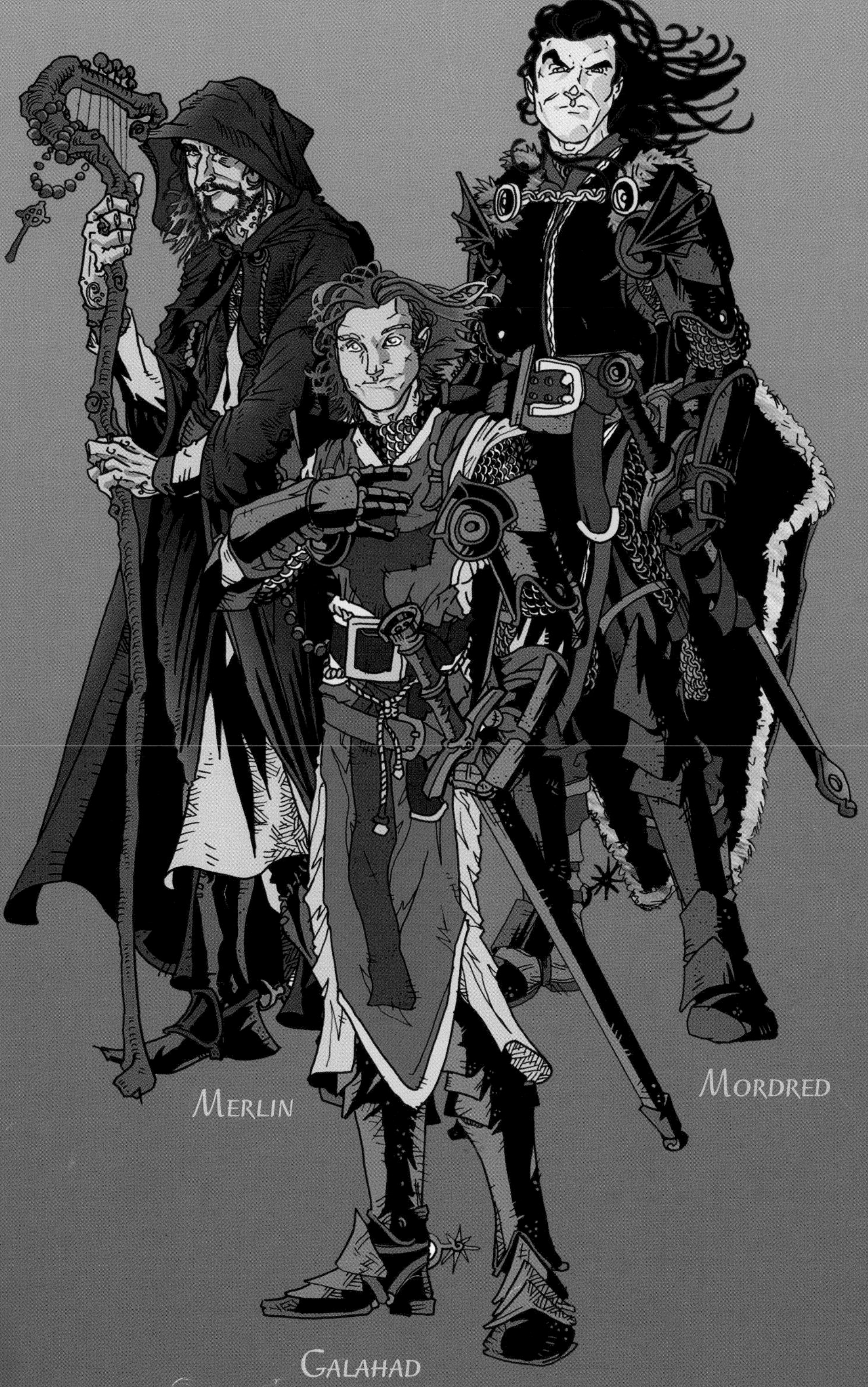
Merlin
Mordred
Galahad

CHAPTER 1

Long ago, in a dark time, two mighty armies fought.

Uther Pendragon, king of Britain, fought Gorlois, the duke of Cornwall. Uther wanted to marry the duke's beautiful wife, Igraine.

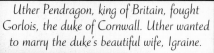

I would give anything to beat my enemy.

Anything, my lord?

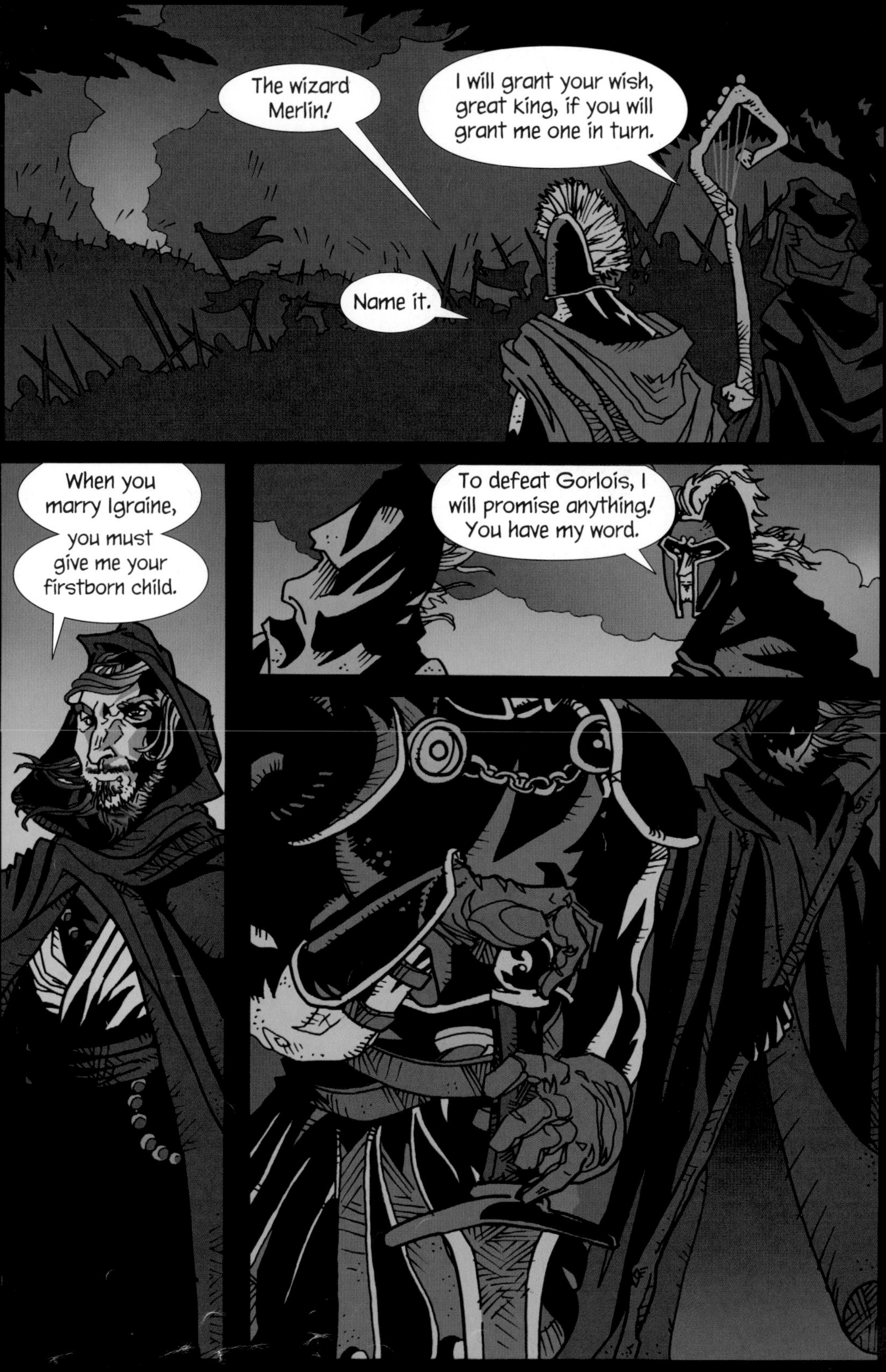
The wizard Merlin!
I will grant your wish, great king, if you will grant me one in turn.
Name it.
When you marry Igraine,
you must give me your firstborn child.
To defeat Gorlois, I will promise anything! You have my word.

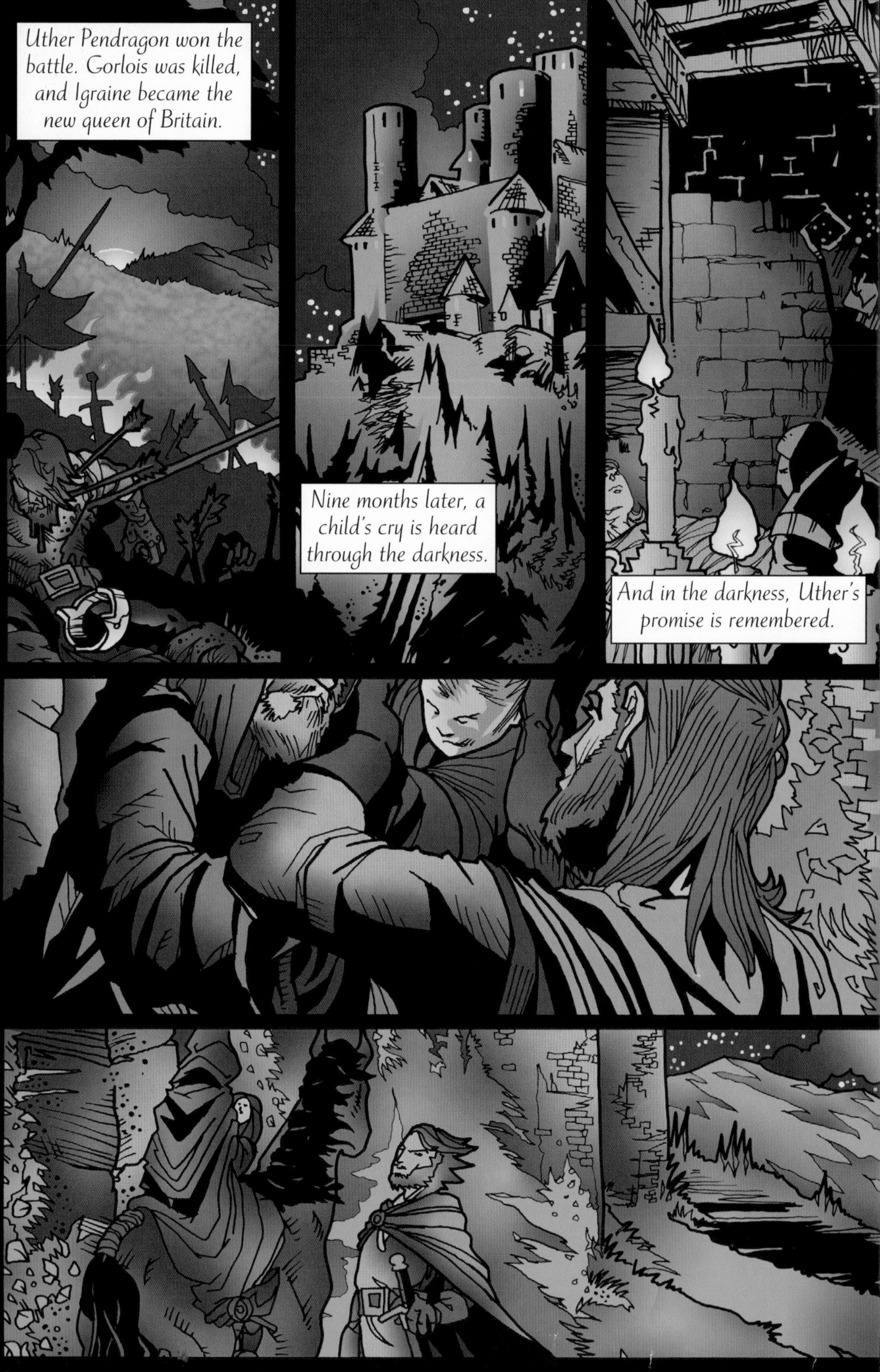
Uther Pendragon won the battle. Gorlois was killed, and Igraine became the new queen of Britain.
Nine months later, a child's cry is heard through the darkness.
And in the darkness, Uther's promise is remembered.

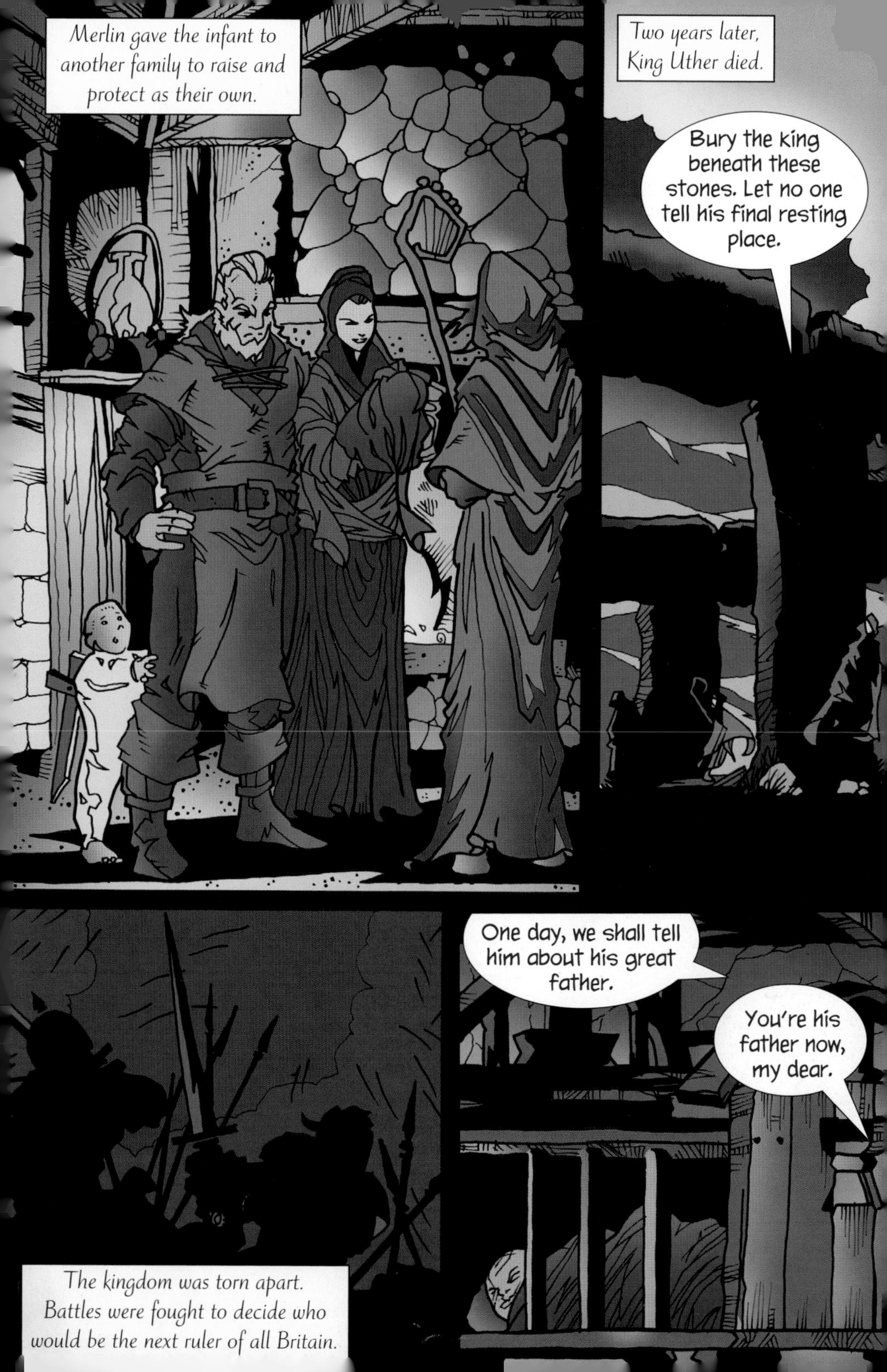

Merlin gave the infant to another family to raise and protect as their own.
Two years later, King Uther died.
Bury the king beneath these stones. Let no one tell his final resting place.
The kingdom was torn apart. Battles were fought to decide who would be the next ruler of all Britain.
One day, we shall tell him about his great father.
You're his father now, my dear.

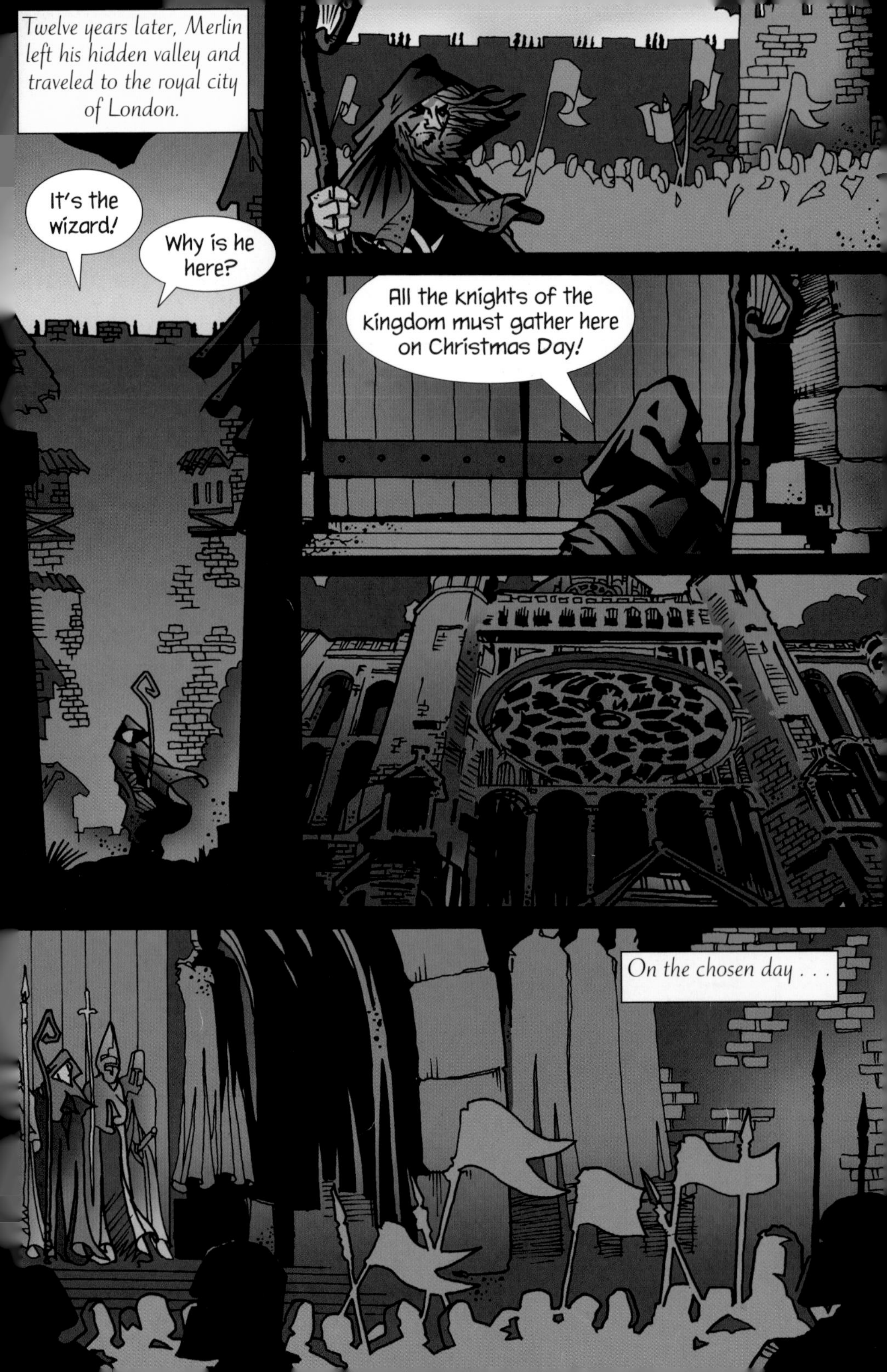
Twelve years later, Merlin left his hidden valley and traveled to the royal city of London.
It's the wizard!
Why is he here?
All the knights of the kingdom must gather here on Christmas Day!
On the chosen day . . .

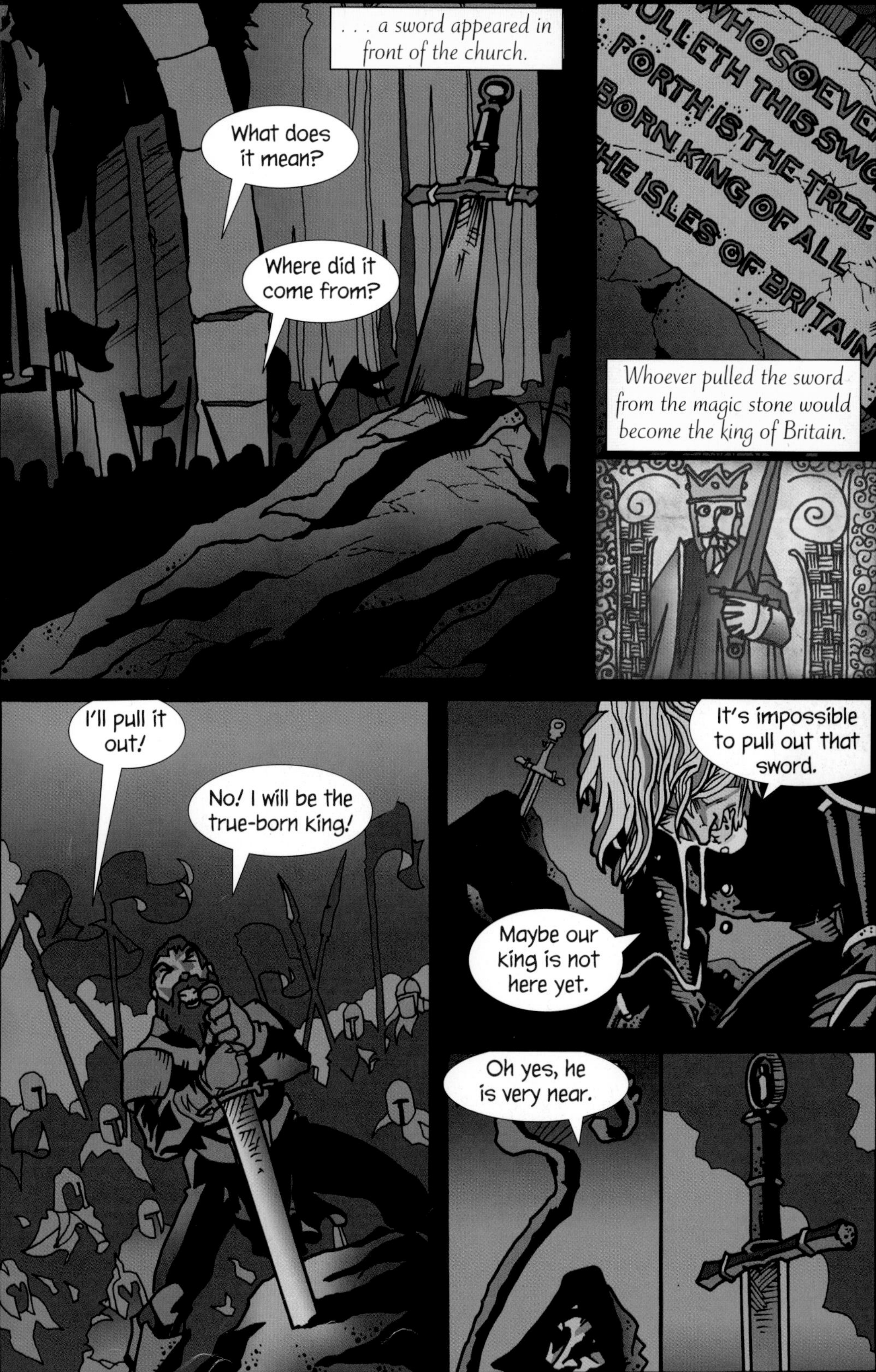
. . . a sword appeared in front of the church.
What does it mean?
Where did it come from?
WHOSOEVE
ULLETH THIS SWO
FORTH IS THE TRUE
BORN KING OF ALL
HE ISLES OF BRITAIN
Whoever pulled the sword from the magic stone would become the king of Britain.
I'll pull it out!
No! I will be the true-born king!
It's impossible to pull out that sword.
Maybe our king is not here yet.
Oh yes, he is very near.

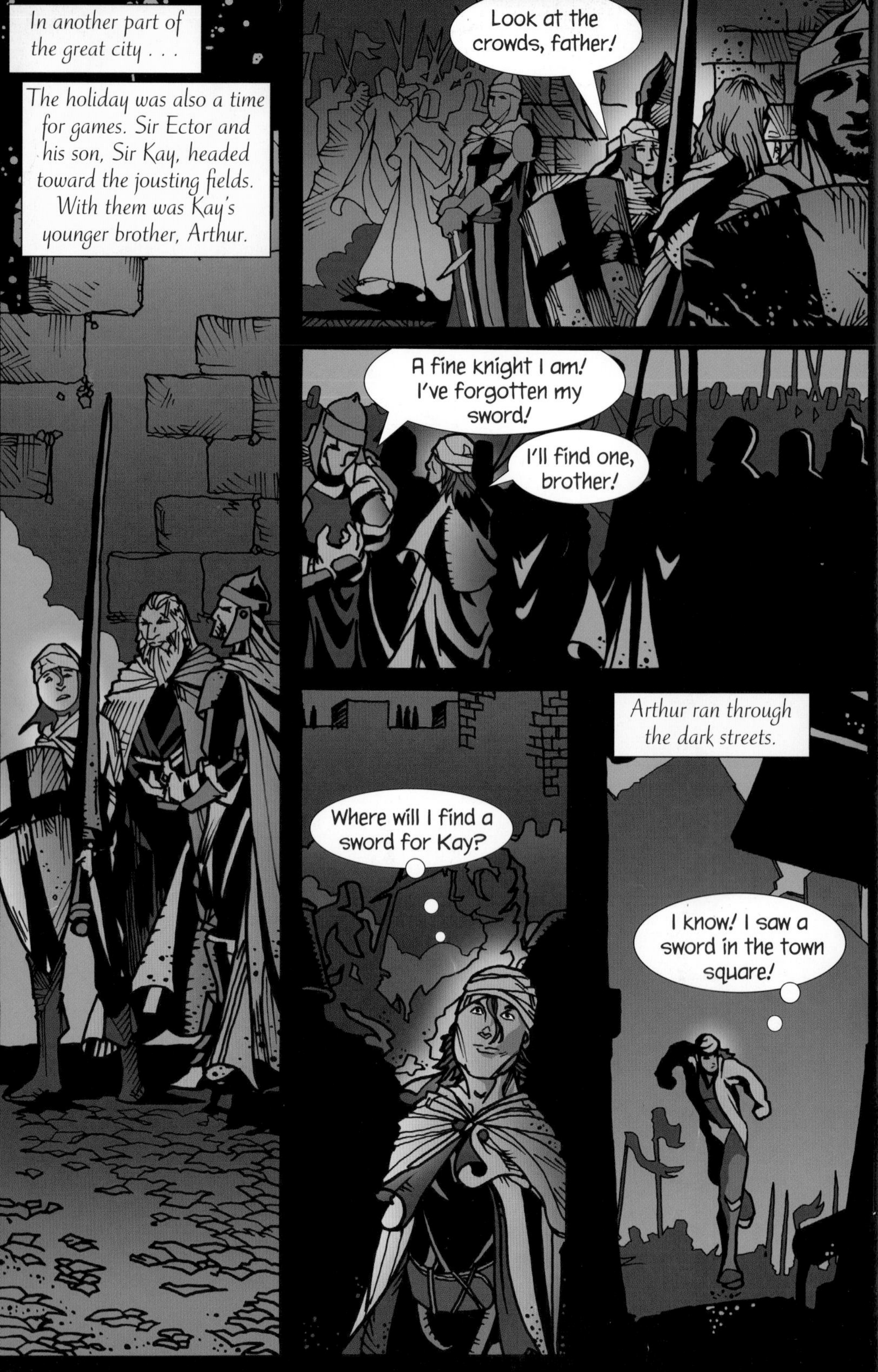
In another part of the great city . . .
The holiday was also a time for games. Sir Ector and his son, Sir Kay, headed toward the jousting fields. With them was Kay's younger brother, Arthur.
Look at the crowds, father!
A fine knight I am! I've forgotten my sword!
I'll find one, brother!
Where will I find a sword for Kay?
Arthur ran through the dark streets.
I know! I saw a sword in the town square!

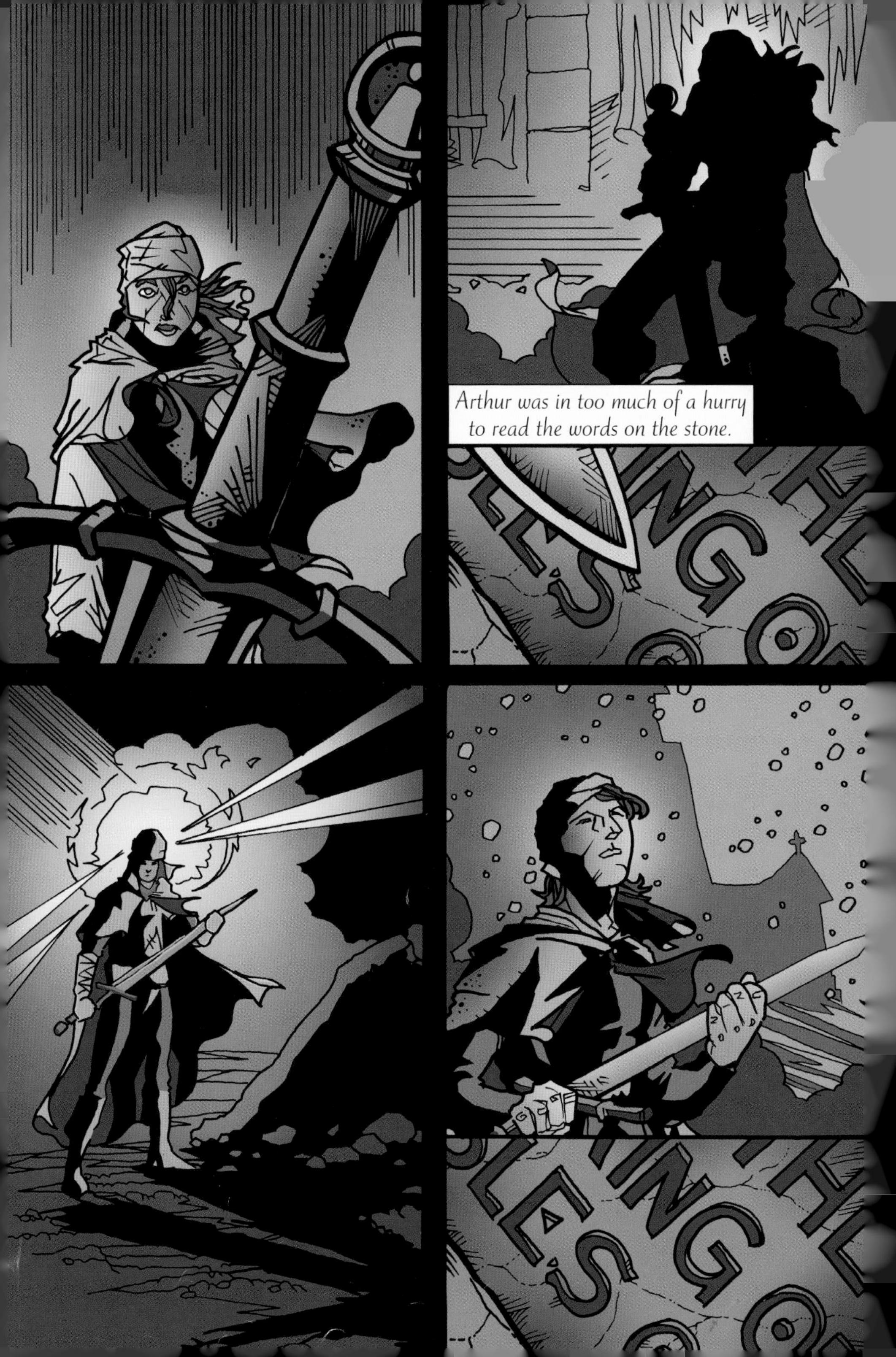
Arthur was in too much of a hurry
to read the words on the stone.

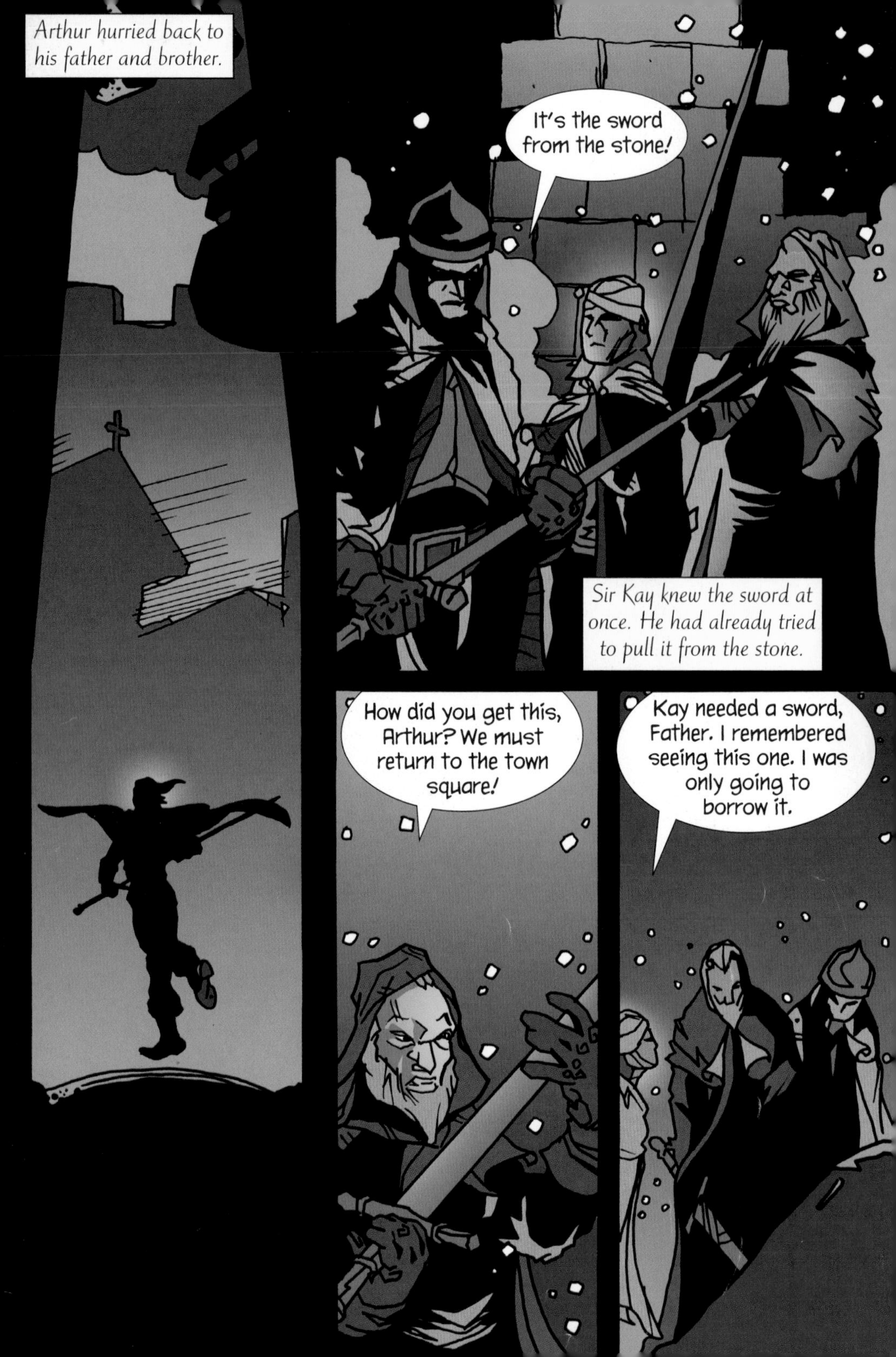
Arthur hurried back to his father and brother.
It's the sword from the stone!
Sir Kay knew the sword at once. He had already tried to pull it from the stone.
How did you get this, Arthur? We must return to the town square!
Kay needed a sword, Father. I remembered seeing this one. I was only going to borrow it.

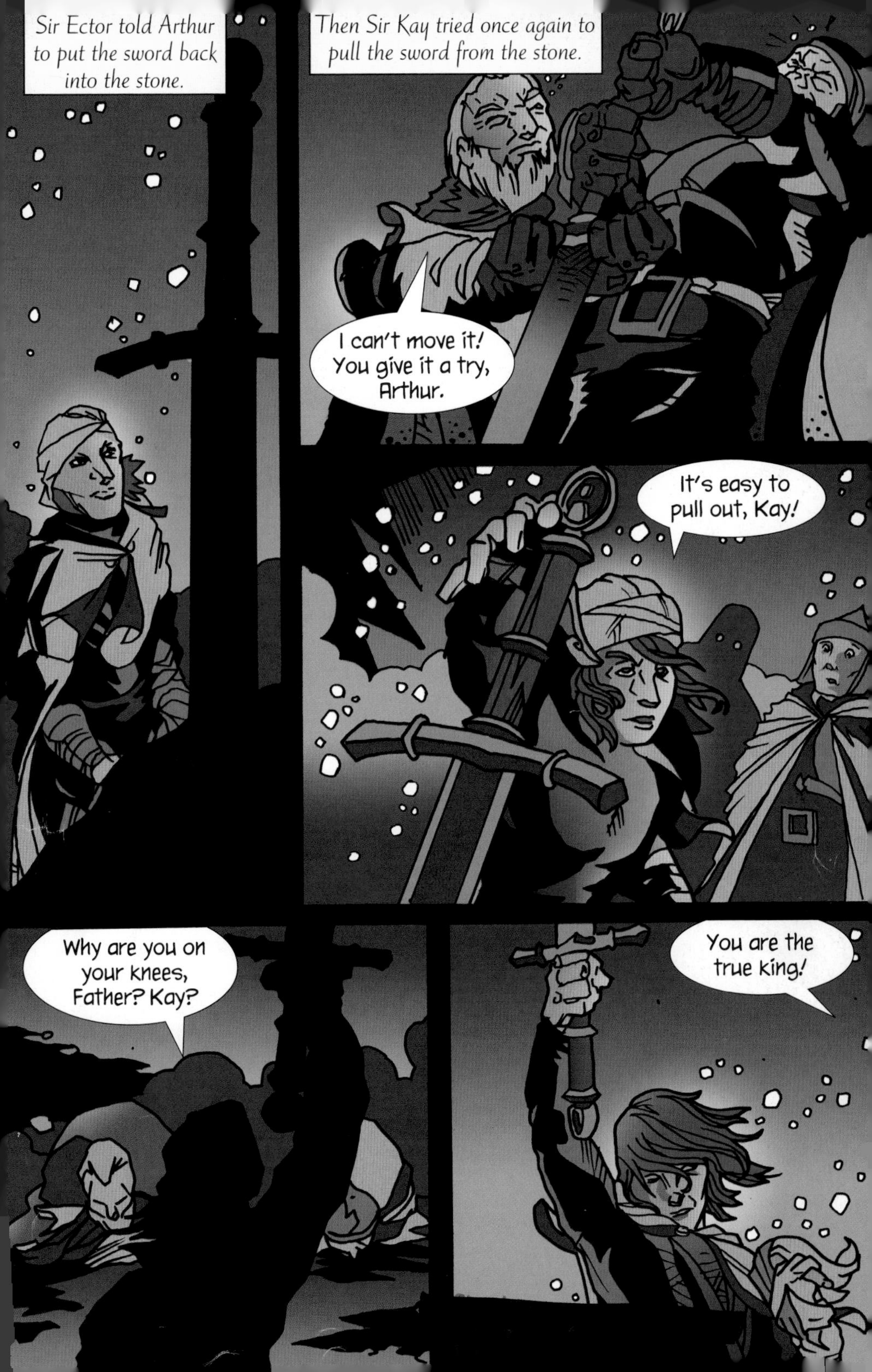
Sir Ector told Arthur to put the sword back into the stone.
Then Sir Kay tried once again to pull the sword from the stone.
I can't move it! You give it a try, Arthur.
It's easy to pull out, Kay!
Why are you on your knees, Father? Kay?
You are the true king!

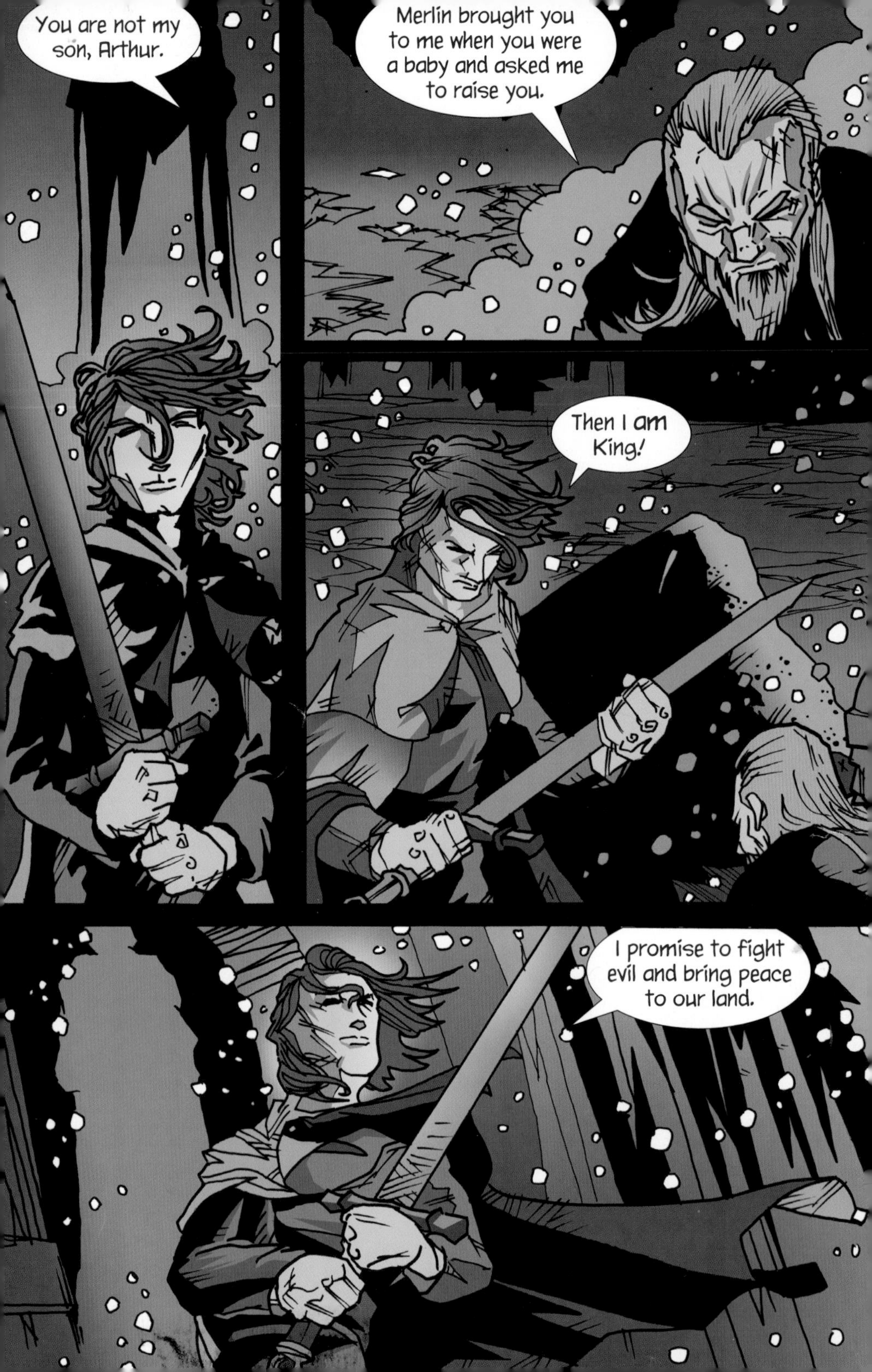
You are not my son, Arthur.
Merlin brought you to me when you were a baby and asked me to raise you.
Then I am King!
I promise to fight evil and bring peace to our land.

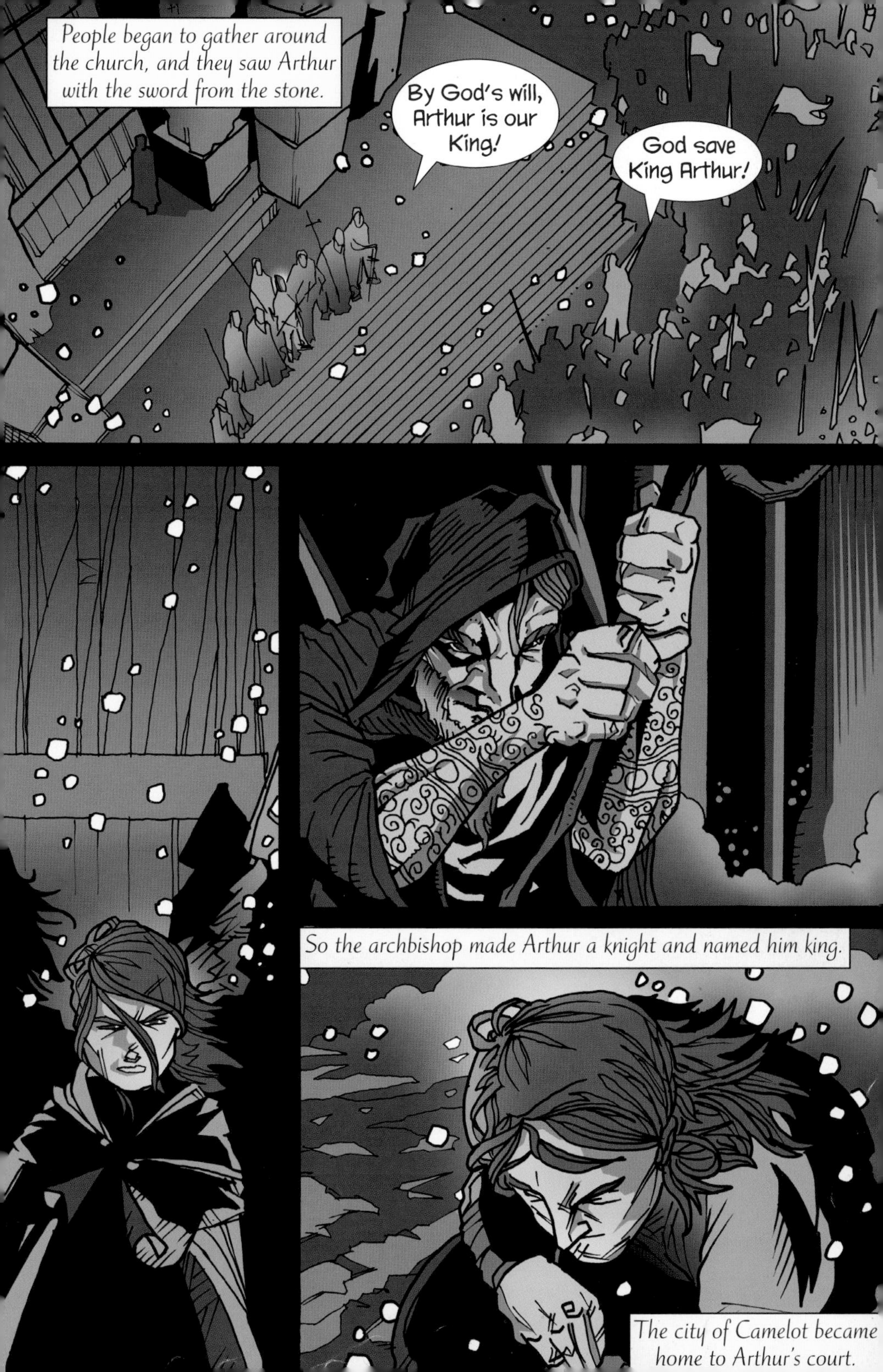
People began to gather around the church, and they saw Arthur with the sword from the stone.
By God's will, Arthur is our King!
God save King Arthur!
So the archbishop made Arthur a knight and named him king.
The city of Camelot became home to Arthur's court.

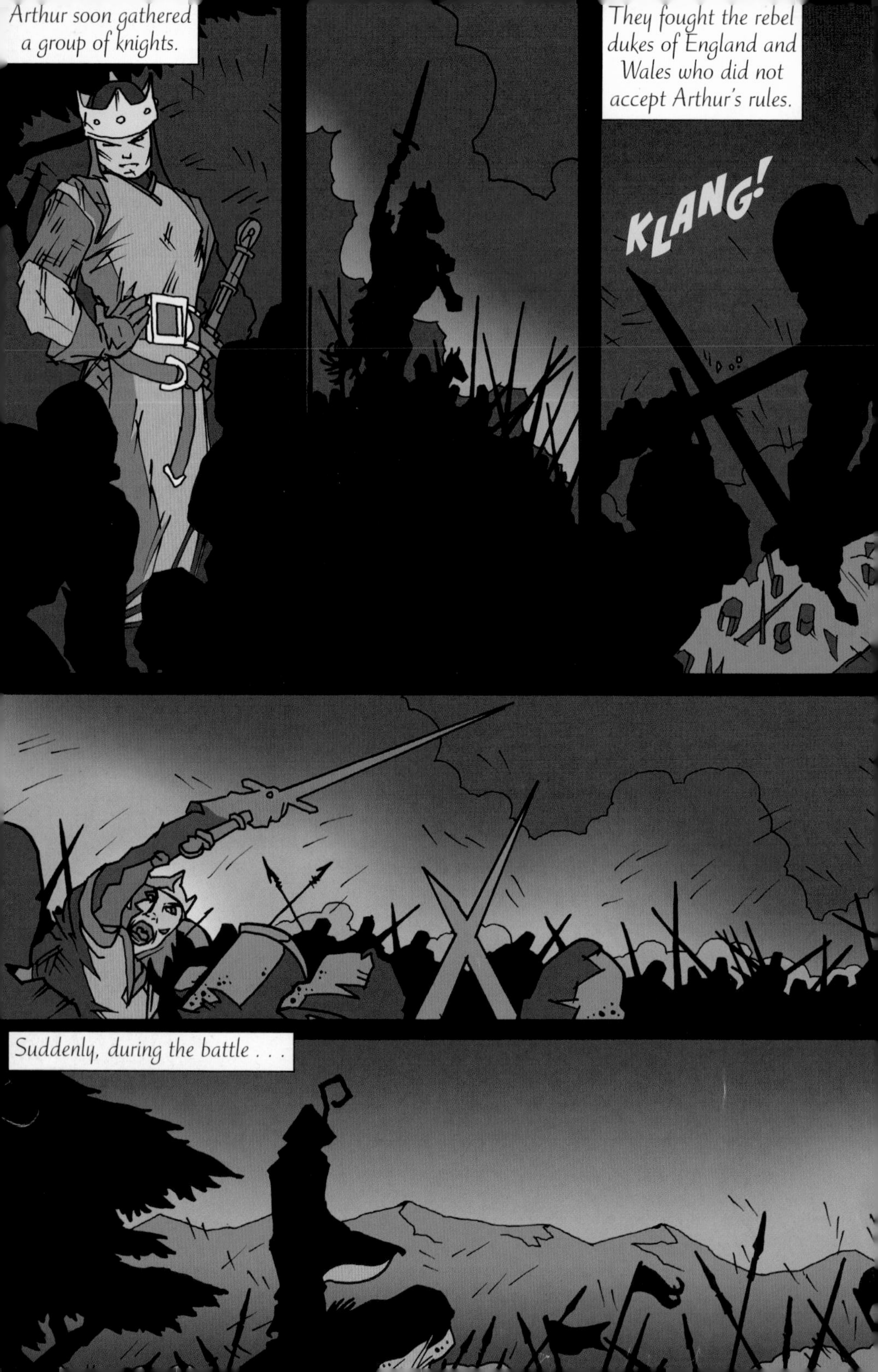

Arthur soon gathered a group of knights.
They fought the rebel dukes of England and Wales who did not accept Arthur's rules.
KLANG!
Suddenly, during the battle . . .

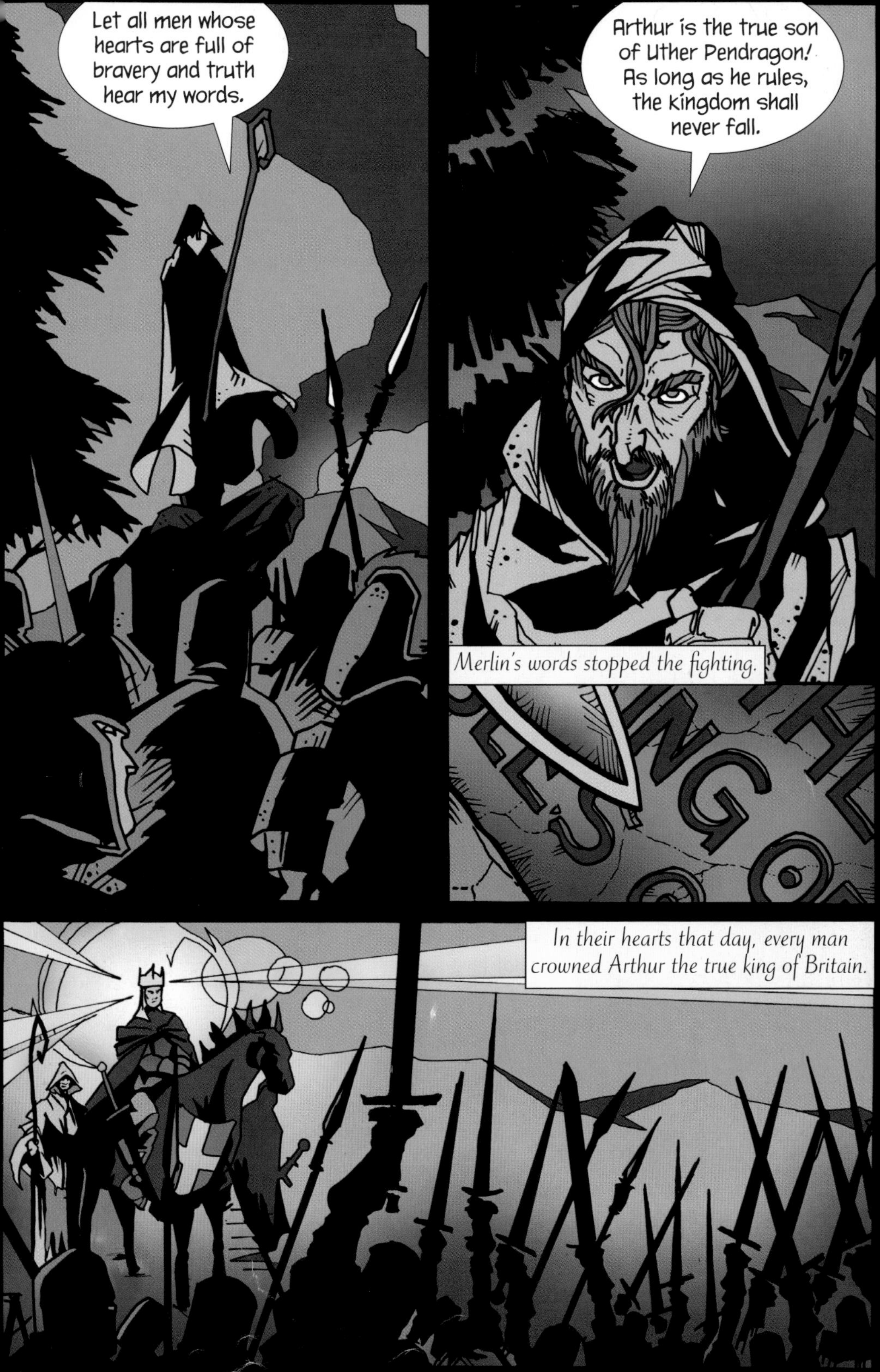
Let all men whose hearts are full of bravery and truth hear my words.
Arthur is the true son of Uther Pendragon! As long as he rules, the kingdom shall never fall.
Merlin's words stopped the fighting.
In their hearts that day, every man crowned Arthur the true king of Britain.

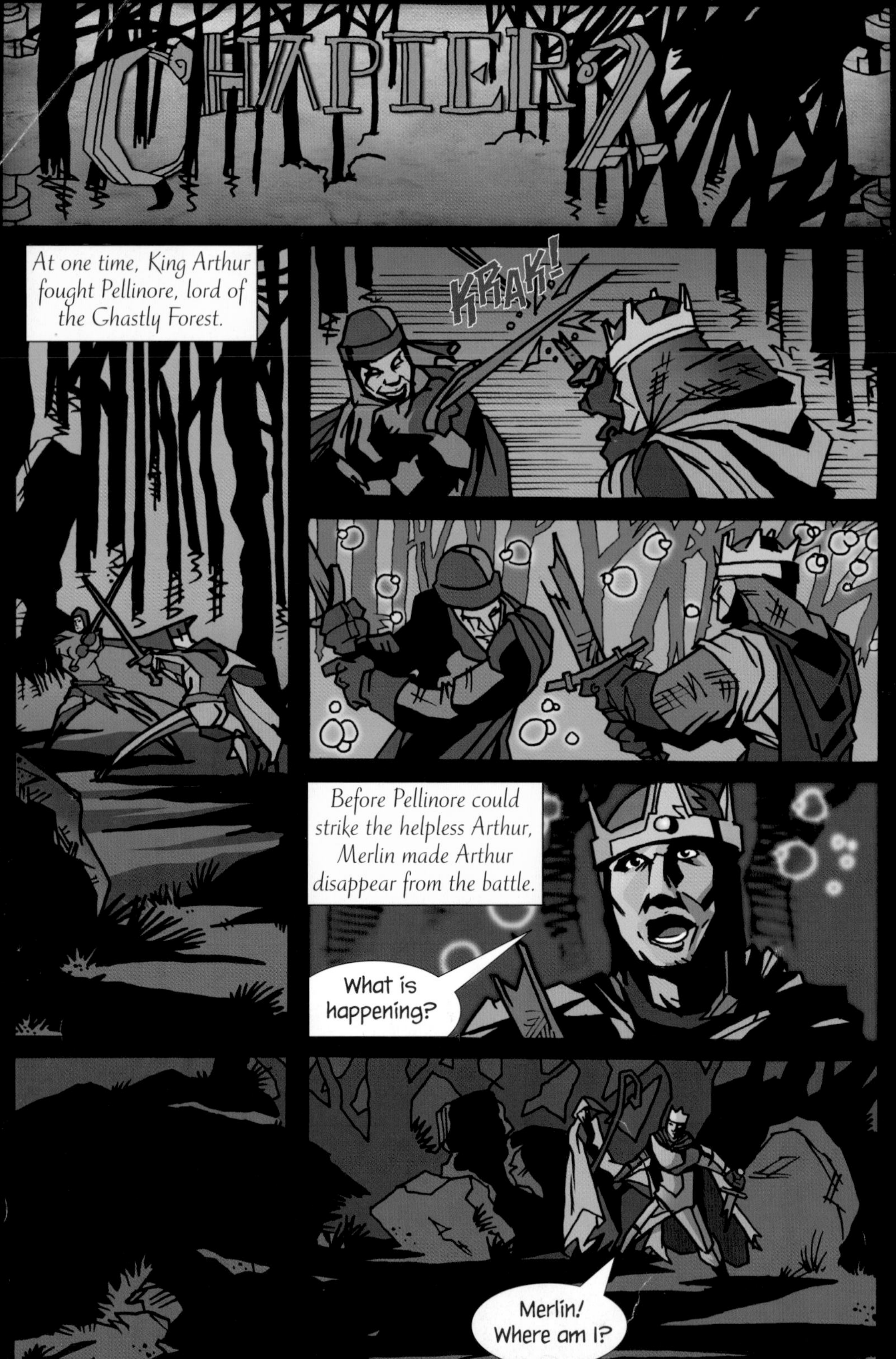
CHAPTER 2
At one time, King Arthur fought Pellinore, lord of the Ghastly Forest.
KRAK!
Before Pellinore could strike the helpless Arthur, Merlin made Arthur disappear from the battle.
What is happening?
Merlin! Where am I?

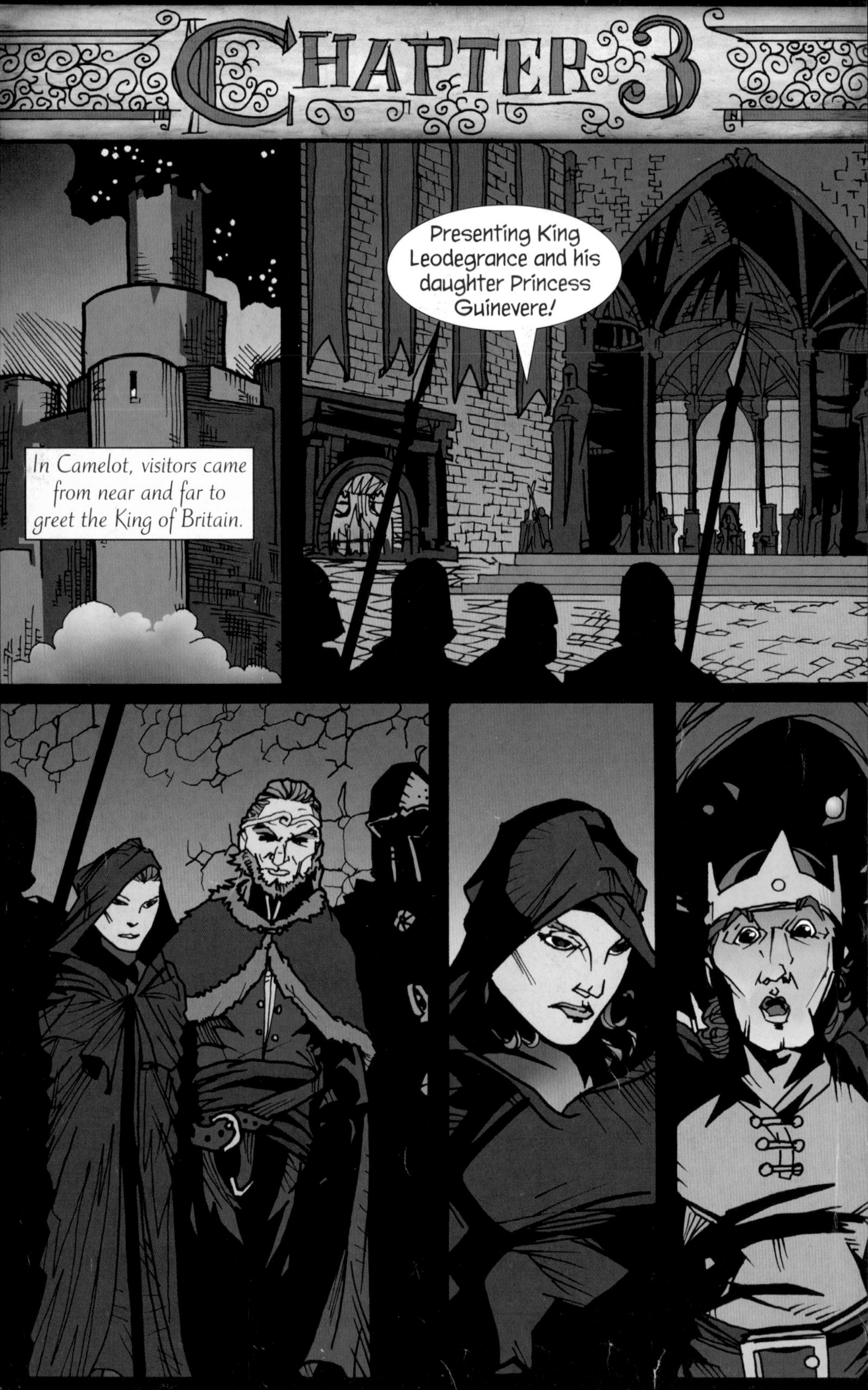
CHAPTER 3
In Camelot, visitors came from near and far to greet the King of Britain.
Presenting King Leodegrance and his daughter Princess Guinevere!

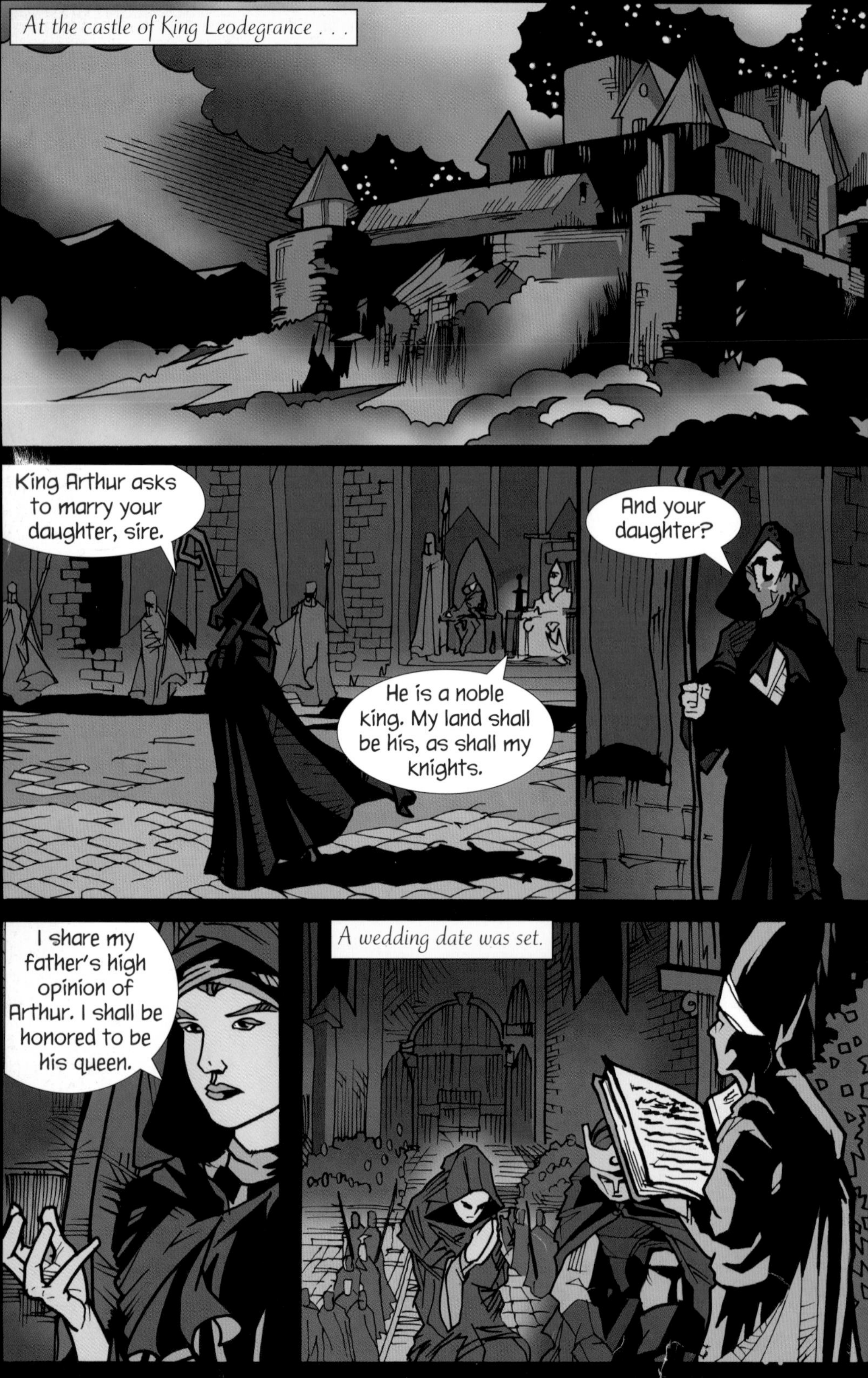
At the castle of King Leodegrance . . .
King Arthur asks to marry your daughter, sire.
He is a noble king. My land shall be his, as shall my knights.
And your daughter?
I share my father's high opinion of Arthur. I shall be honored to be his queen.
A wedding date was set.

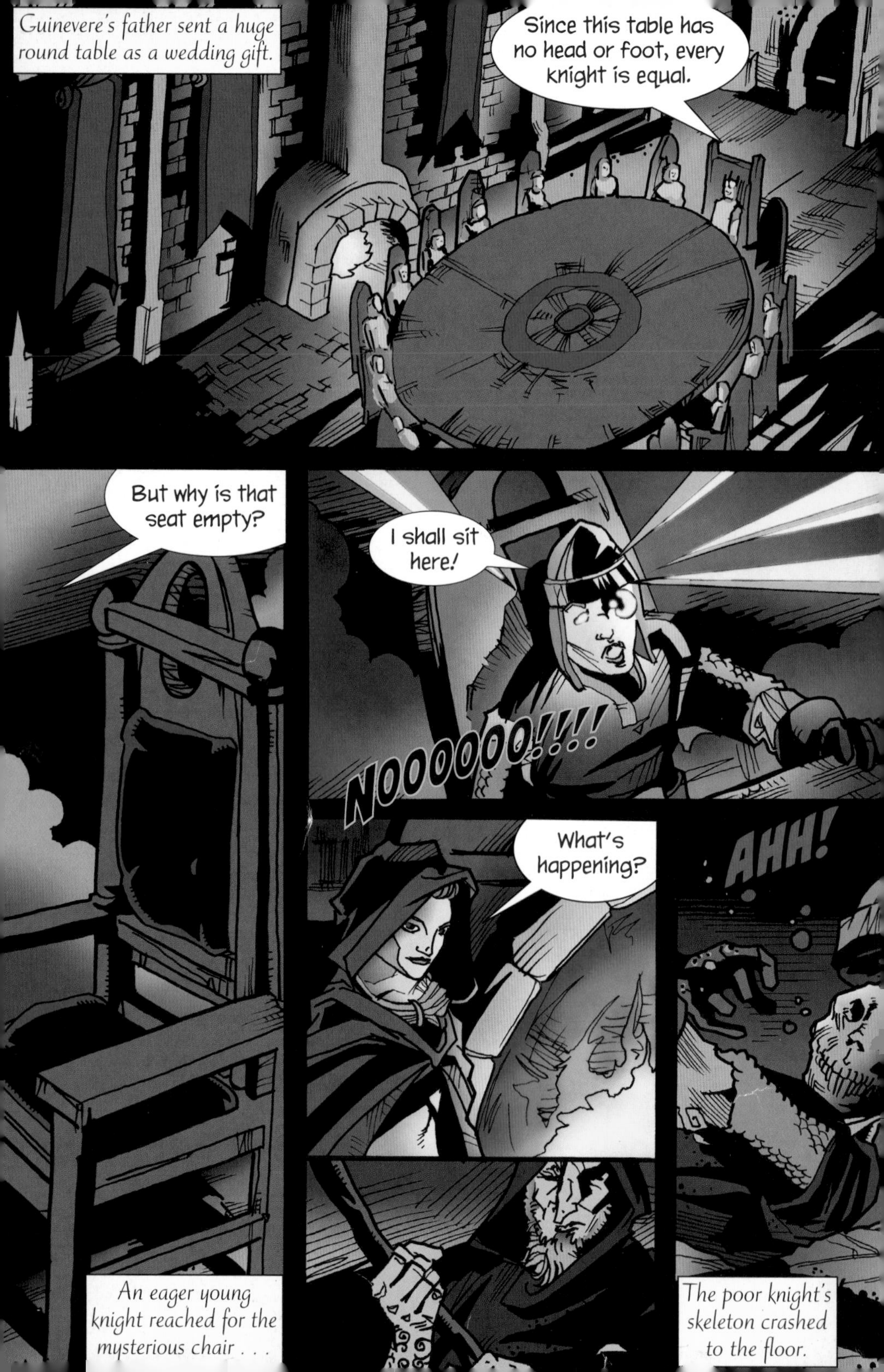
Guinevere's father sent a huge round table as a wedding gift.
Since this table has no head or foot, every knight is equal.
But why is that seat empty?
I shall sit here!
NOOOOOO!!!!
What's happening?
AHH!
An eager young knight reached for the mysterious chair . . .
The poor knight's skeleton crashed to the floor.

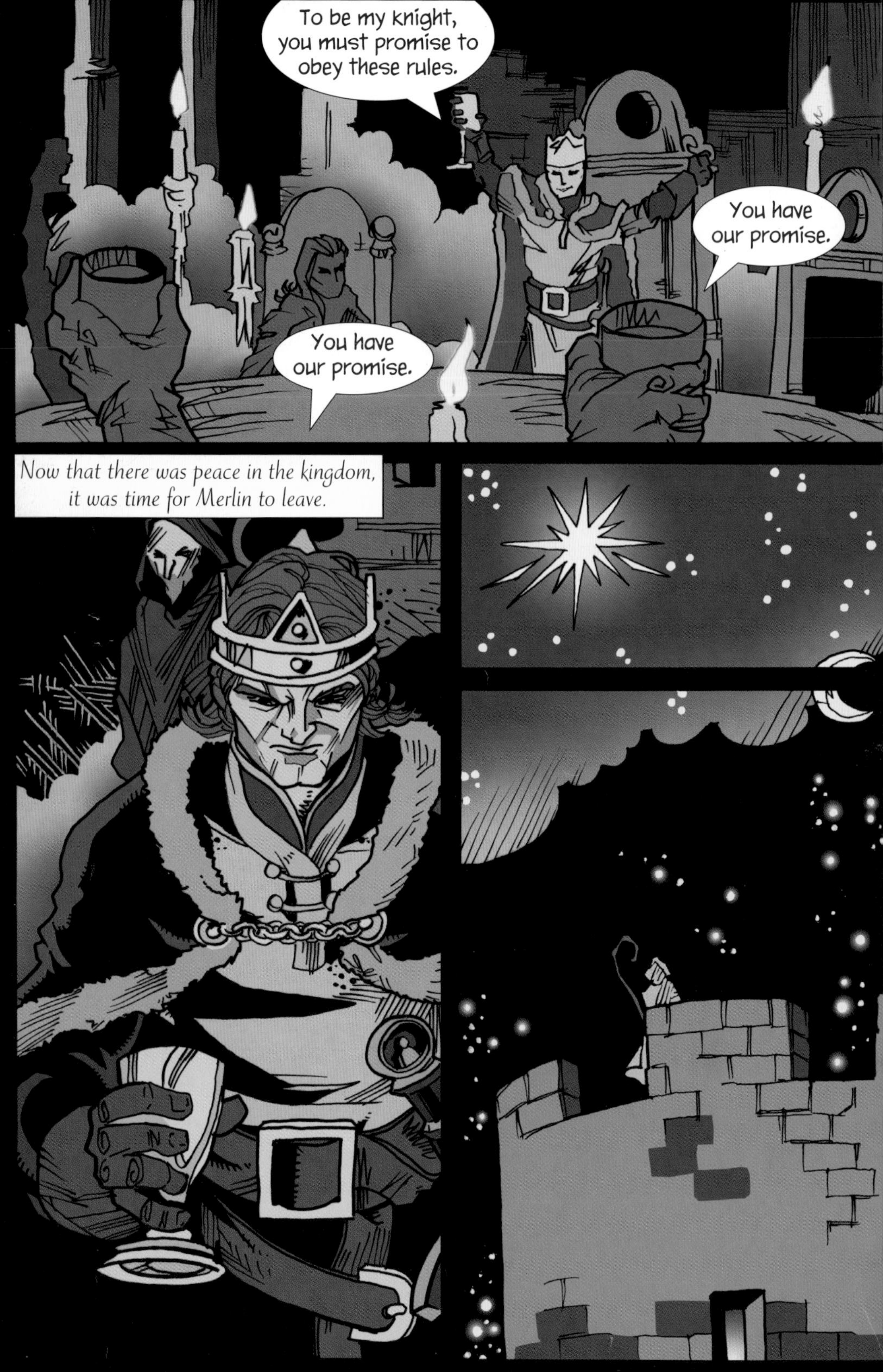
To be my knight, you must promise to obey these rules.
You have our promise.
You have our promise.
Now that there was peace in the kingdom, it was time for Merlin to leave.

Chapter 4

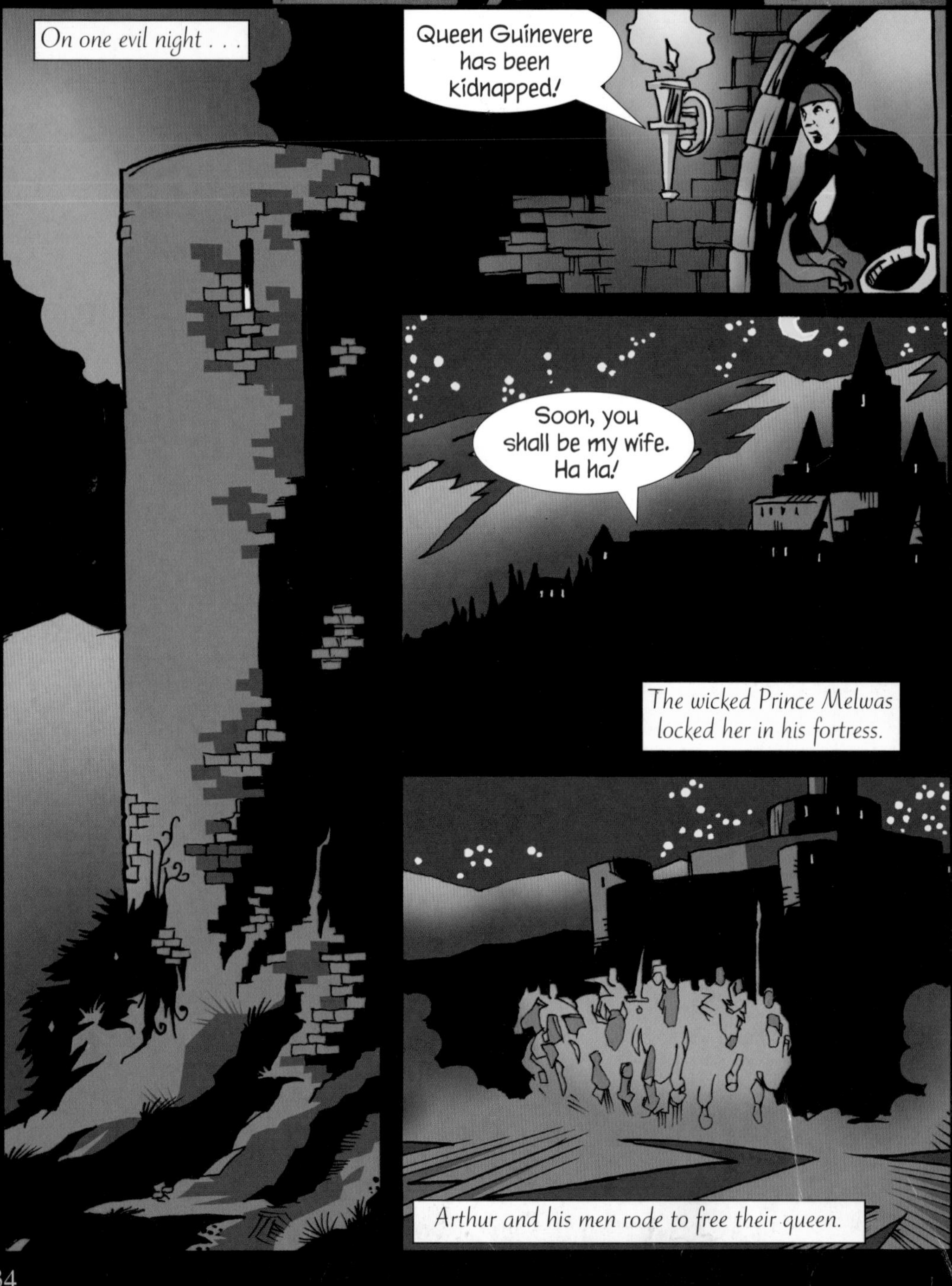

On one evil night . . .
Queen Guinevere has been kidnapped!
Soon, you shall be my wife. Ha ha!
The wicked Prince Melwas locked her in his fortress.
Arthur and his men rode to free their queen.

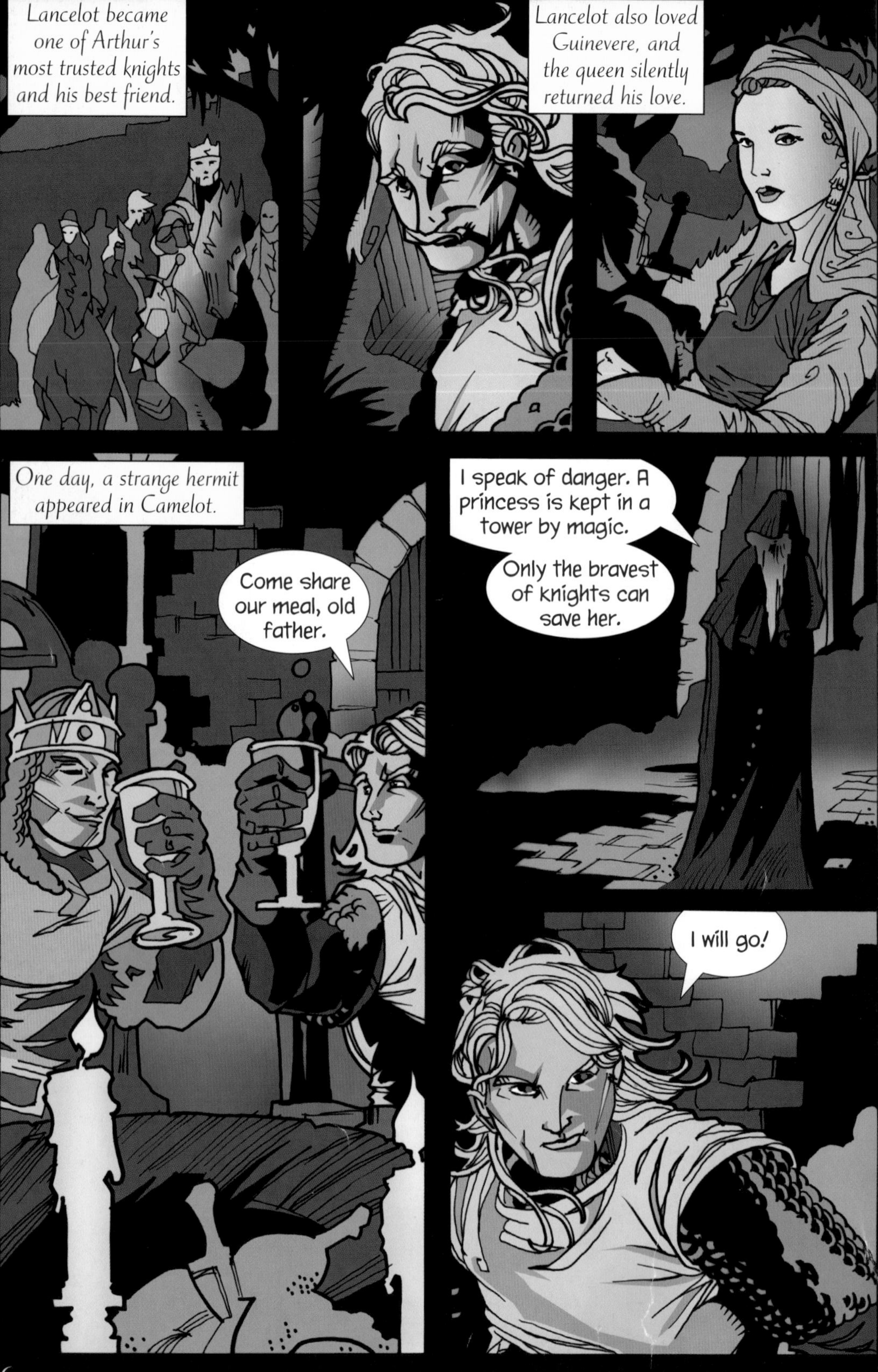
Lancelot became one of Arthur's most trusted knights and his best friend.
Lancelot also loved Guinevere, and the queen silently returned his love.
One day, a strange hermit appeared in Camelot.
Come share our meal, old father.
I speak of danger. A princess is kept in a tower by magic.
Only the bravest of knights can save her.
I will go!

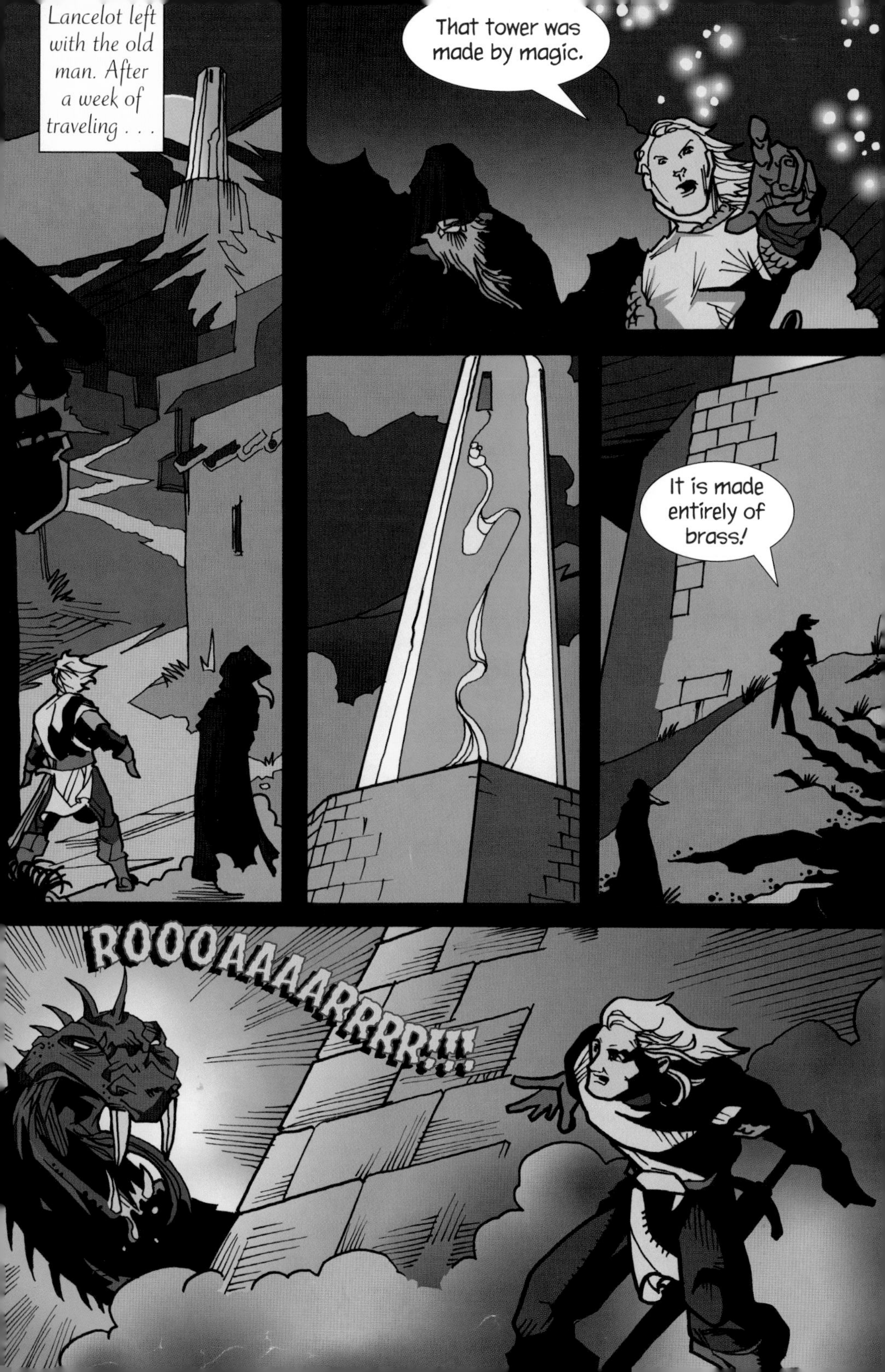
Lancelot left with the old man. After a week of traveling . . .
That tower was made by magic.
It is made entirely of brass!
ROOOAAAARRRRR!!!

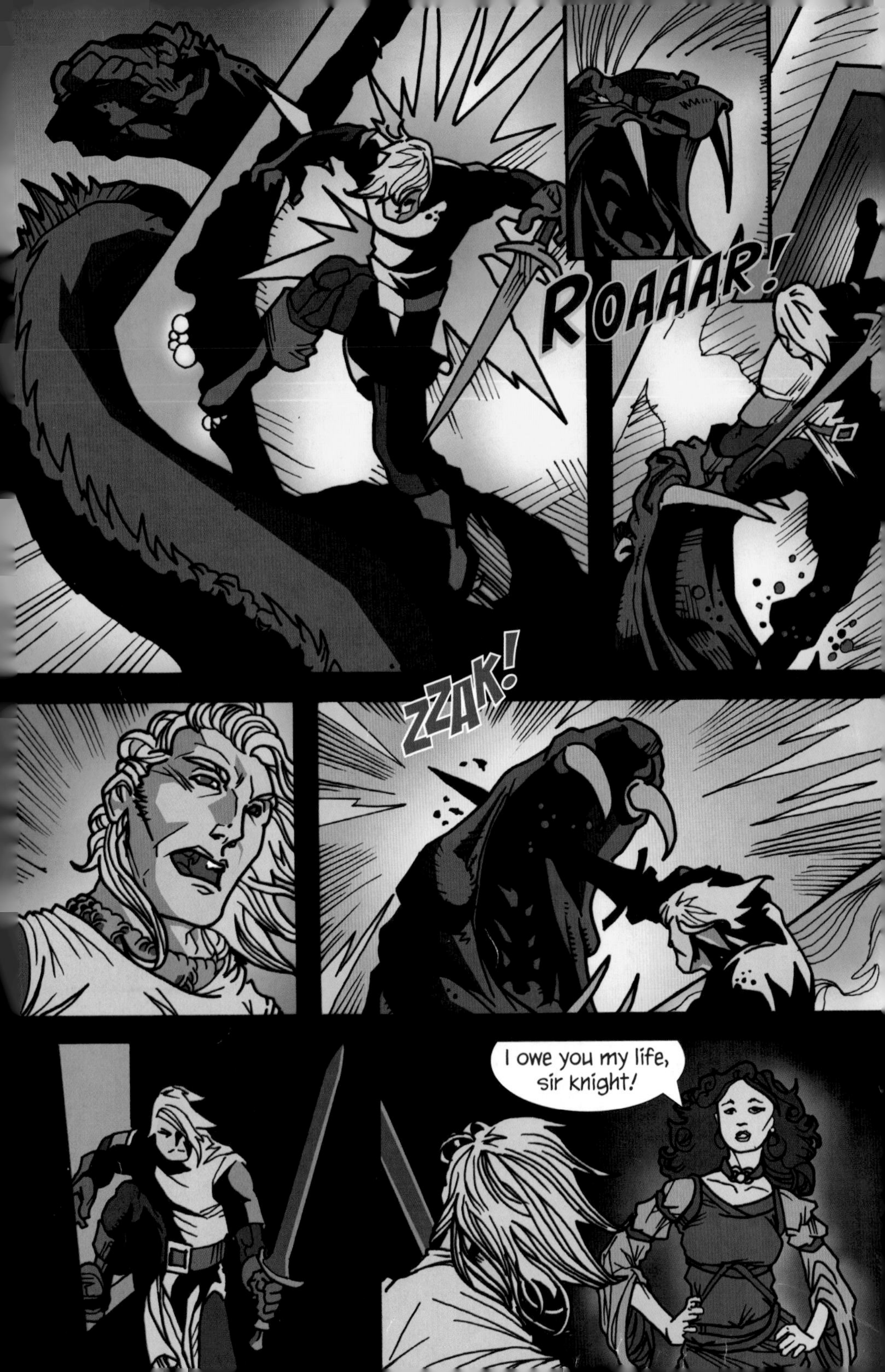
ROAAAR!
ZZAK!
I owe you my life, sir knight!

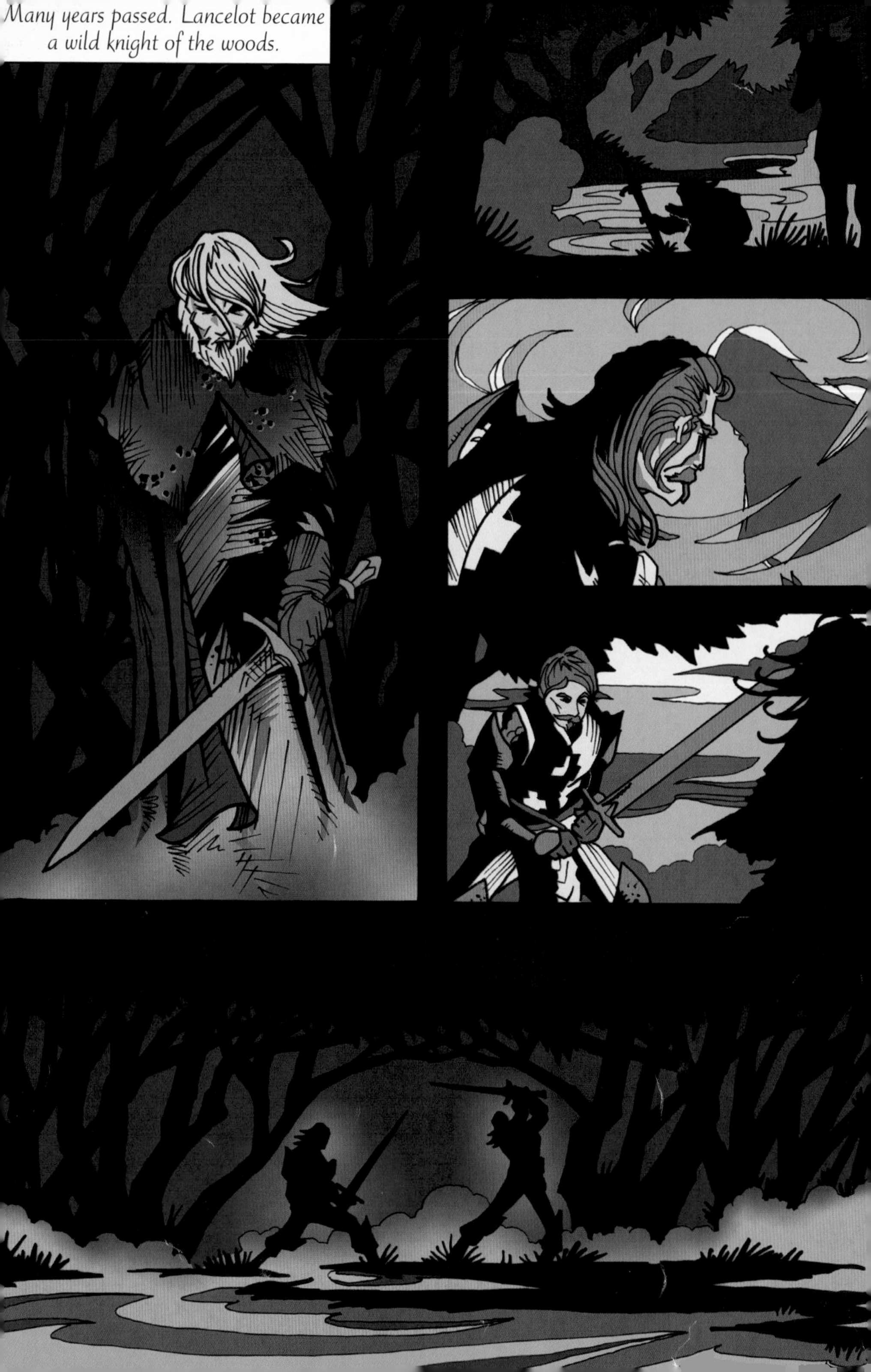
Many years passed. Lancelot became a wild knight of the woods.

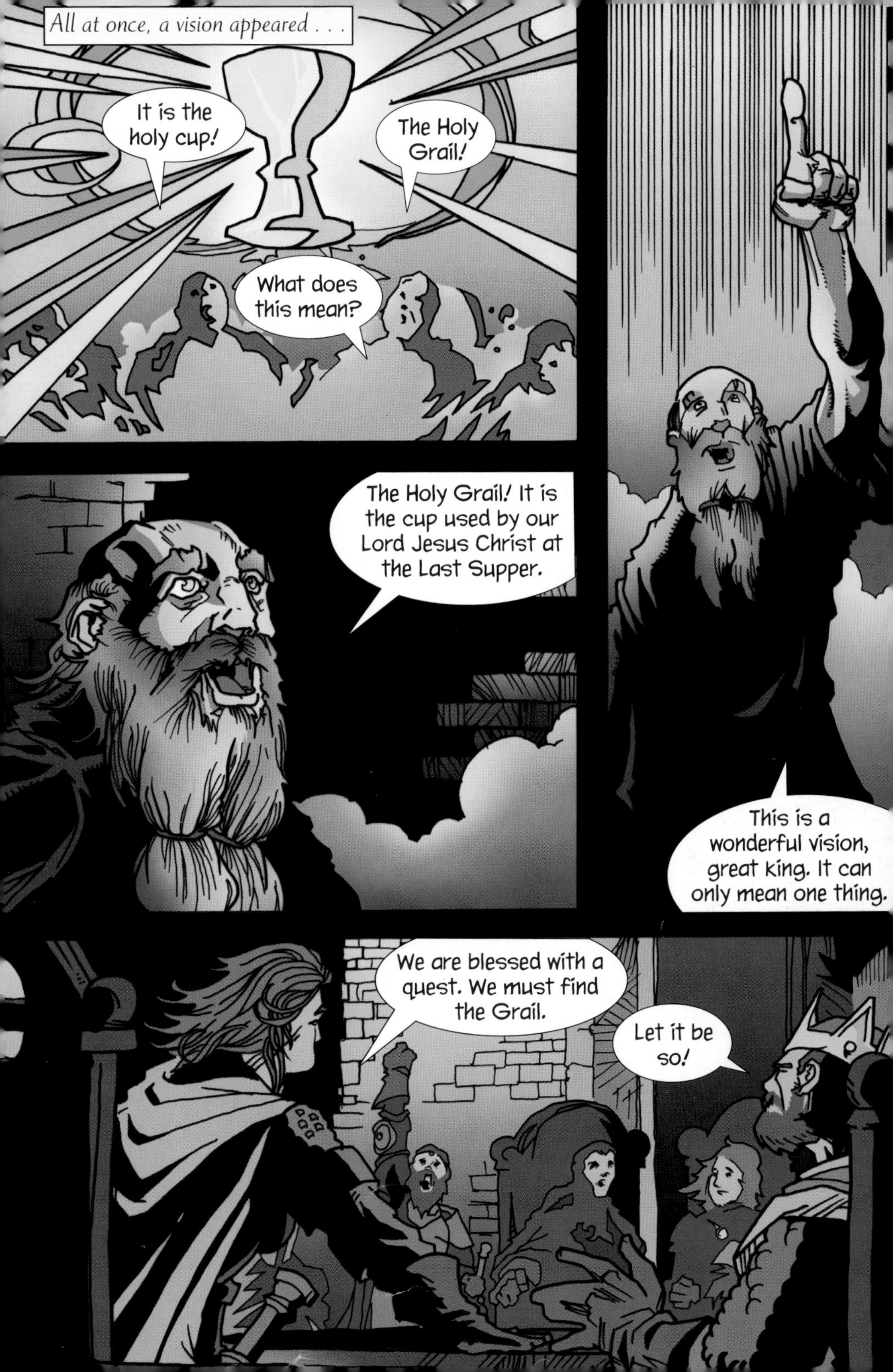
All at once, a vision appeared . . .
It is the holy cup!
The Holy Grail!
What does this mean?
The Holy Grail! It is the cup used by our Lord Jesus Christ at the Last Supper.
This is a wonderful vision, great king. It can only mean one thing.
We are blessed with a quest. We must find the Grail.
Let it be so!

Galahad drank from the cup, and then . . .

Galahad and the Grail were never seen again.

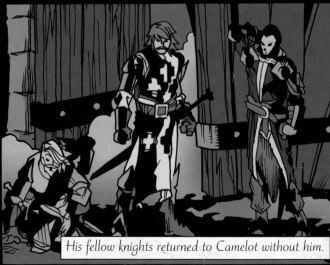

His fellow knights returned to Camelot without him.

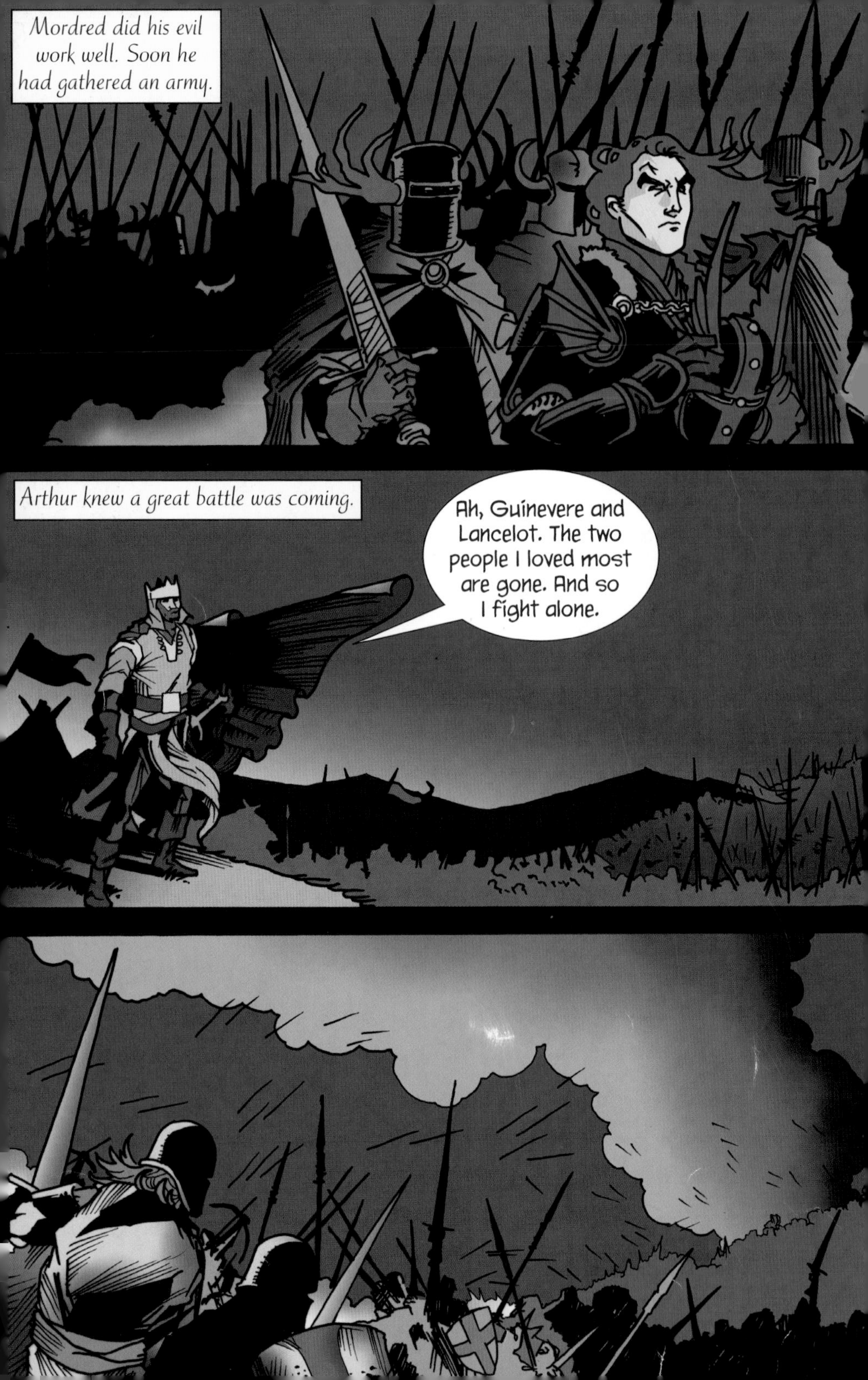
Mordred did his evil work well. Soon he had gathered an army.
Arthur knew a great battle was coming.
Ah, Guinevere and Lancelot. The two people I loved most are gone. And so I fight alone.

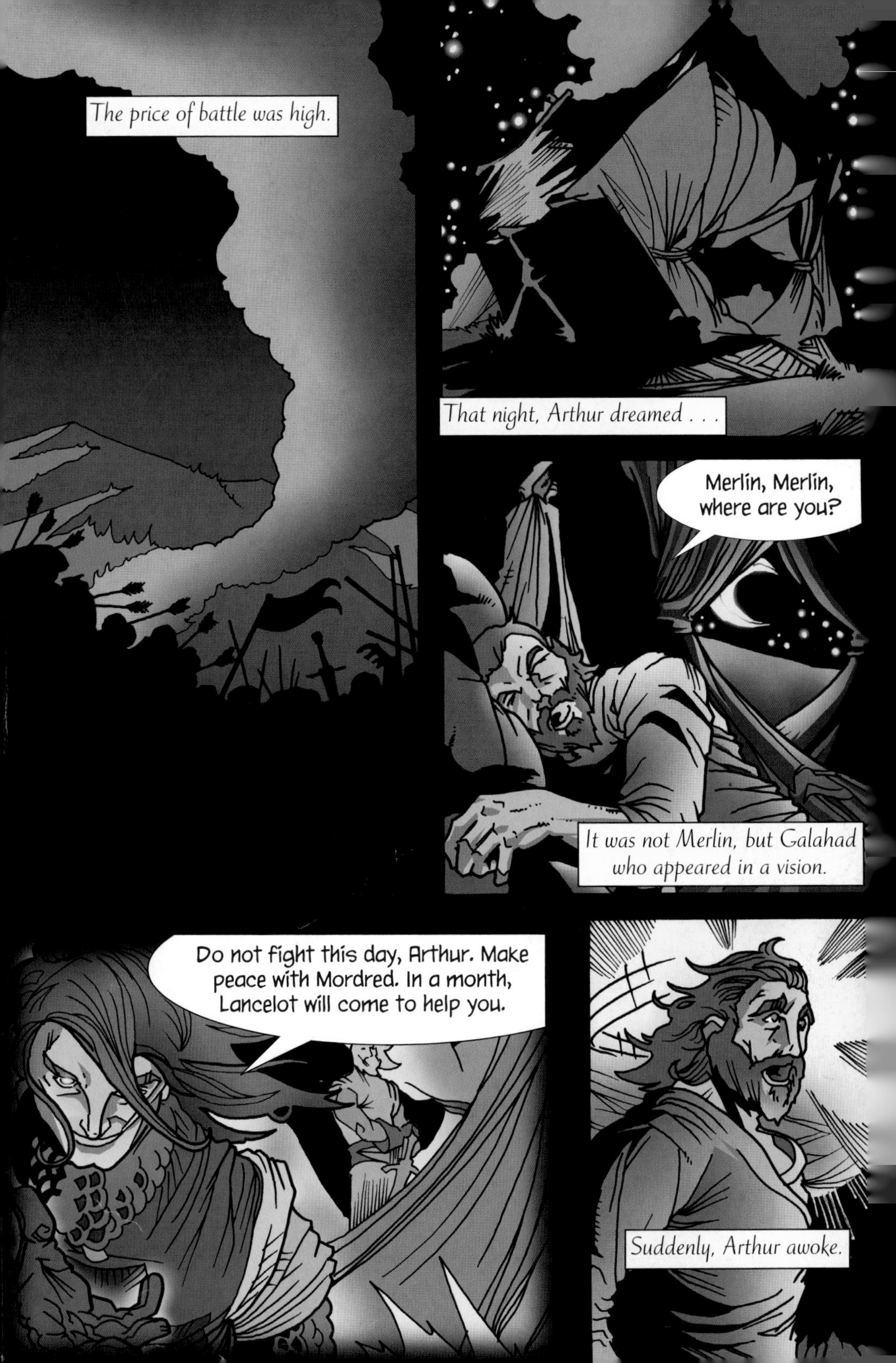
The price of battle was high.
That night, Arthur dreamed . . .
Merlin, Merlin, where are you?
It was not Merlin, but Galahad who appeared in a vision.
Do not fight this day, Arthur. Make peace with Mordred. In a month, Lancelot will come to help you.
Suddenly, Arthur awoke.

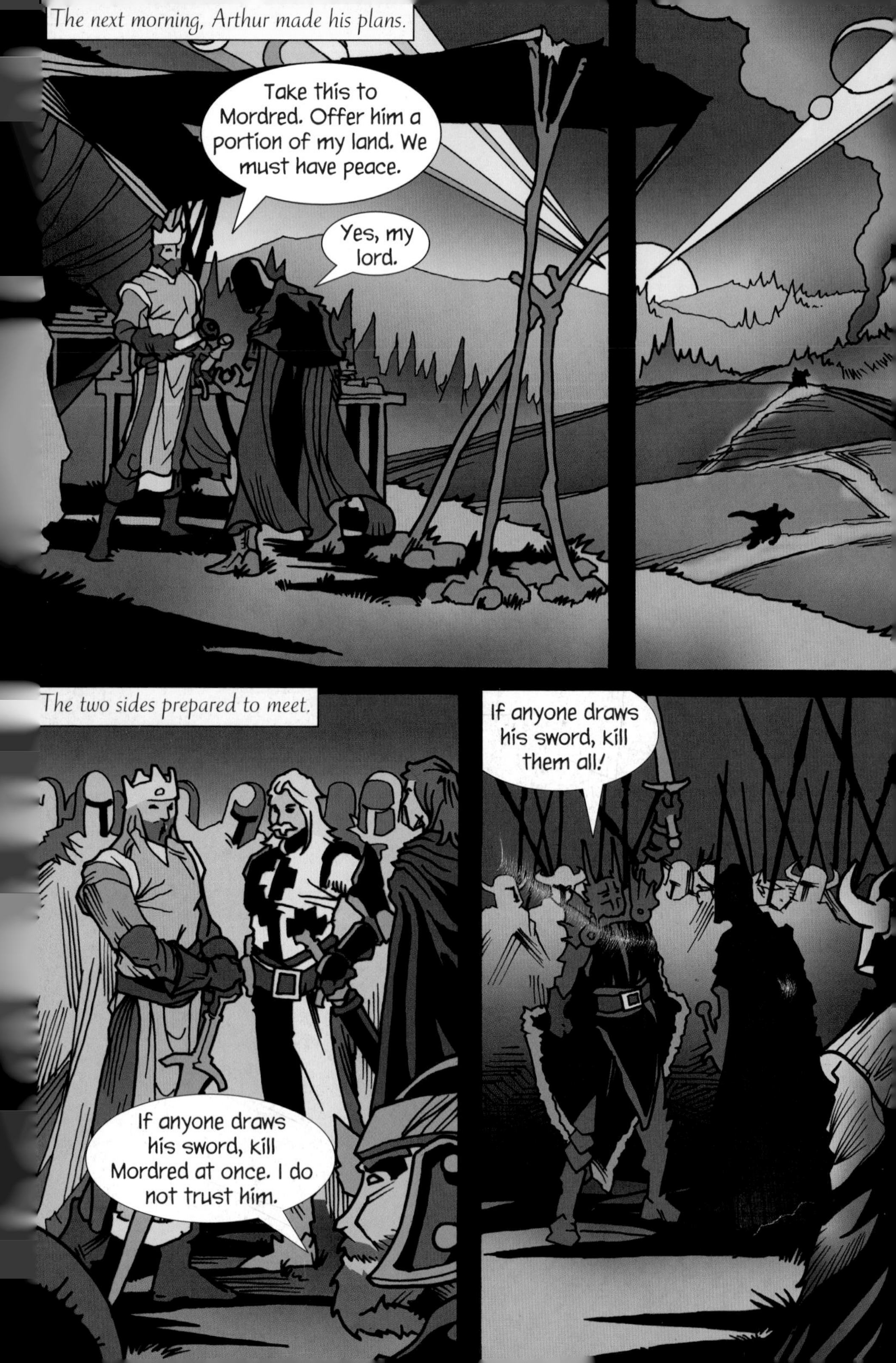
The next morning, Arthur made his plans.
Take this to Mordred. Offer him a portion of my land. We must have peace.
Yes, my lord.
The two sides prepared to meet.
If anyone draws his sword, kill Mordred at once. I do not trust him.
If anyone draws his sword, kill them all!

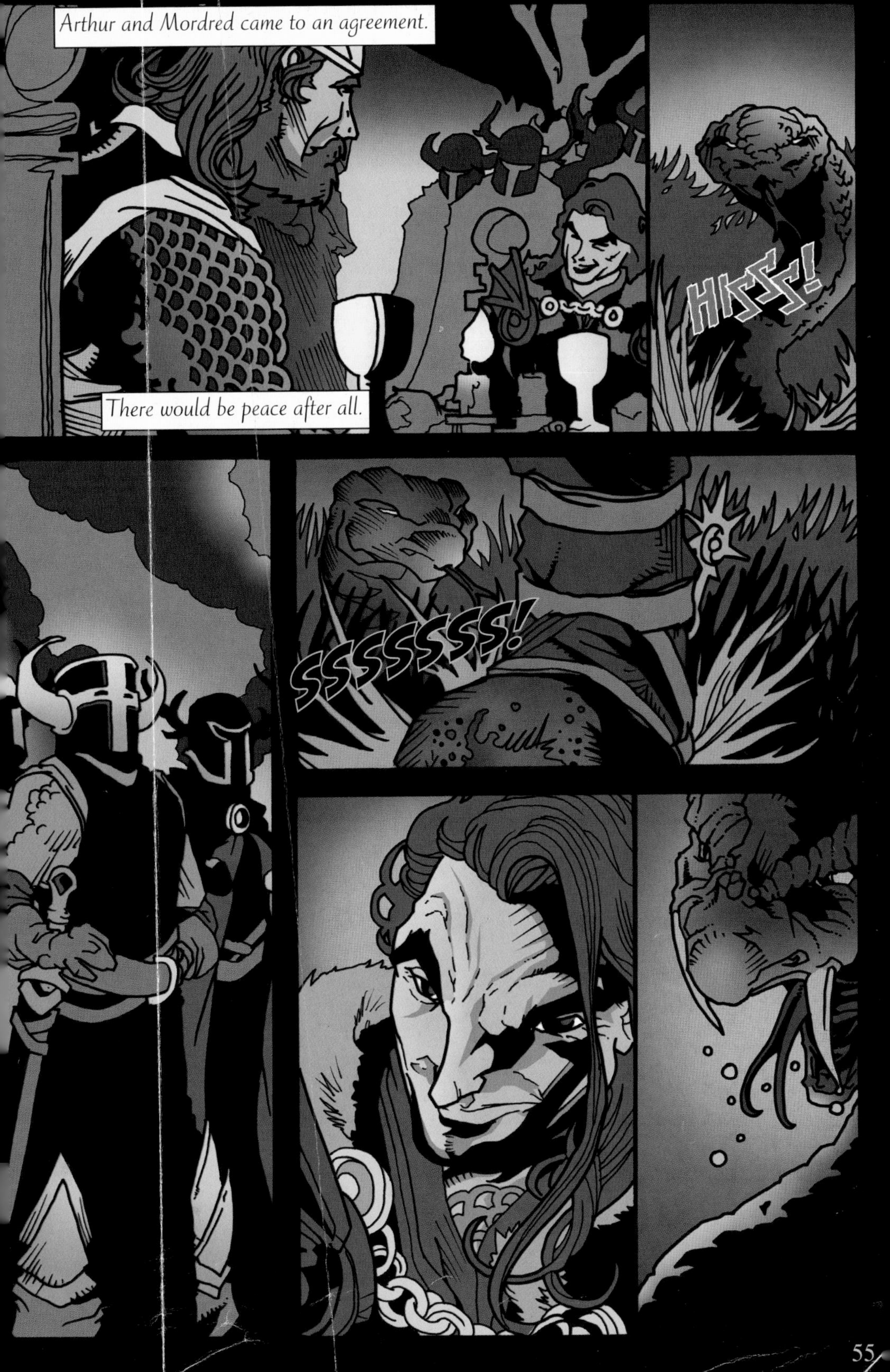
Arthur and Mordred came to an agreement.
There would be peace after all.
HISSS!
SSSSSSS!

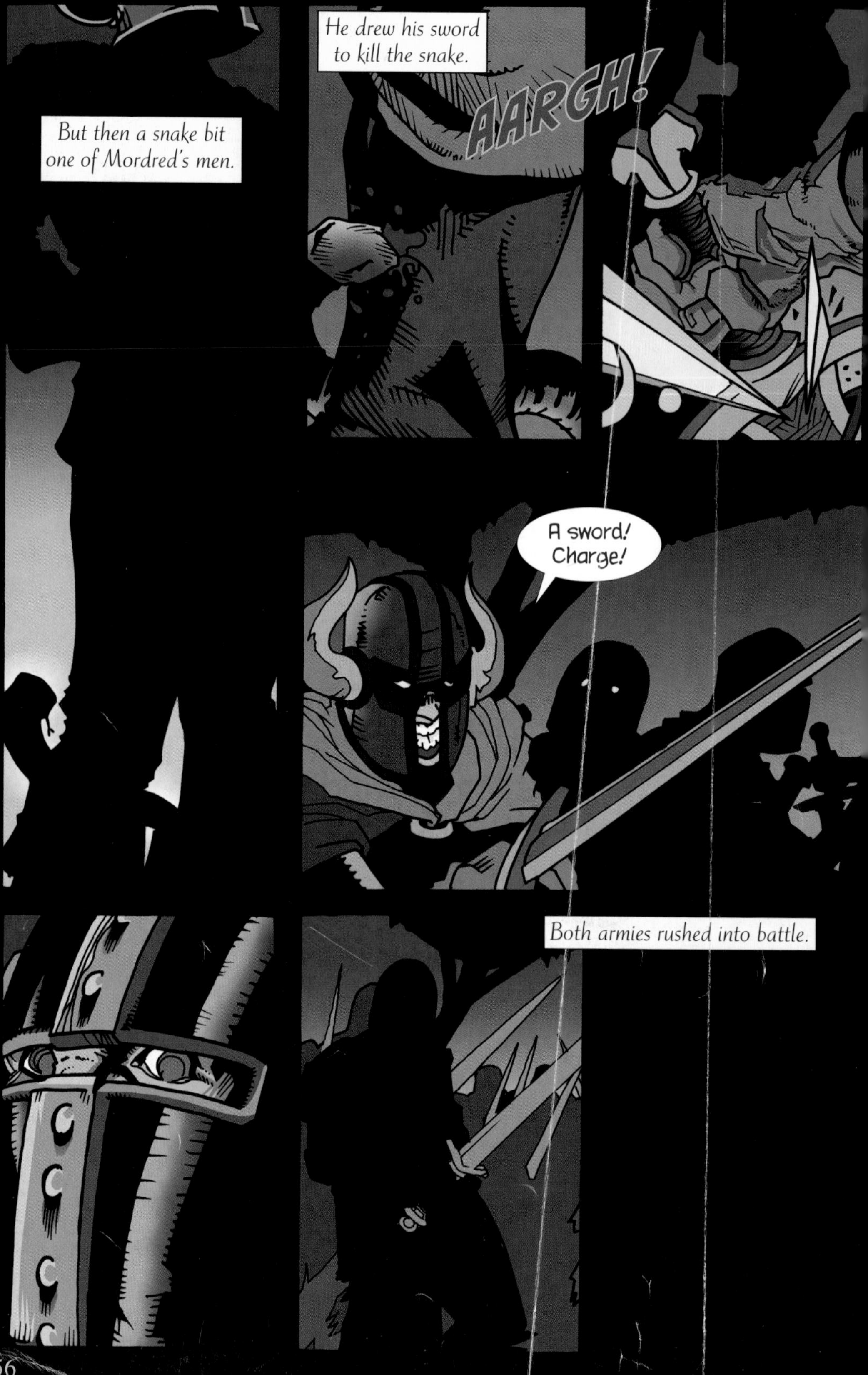
But then a snake bit one of Mordred's men.
He drew his sword to kill the snake.
AARGH!
A sword! Charge!
Both armies rushed into battle.

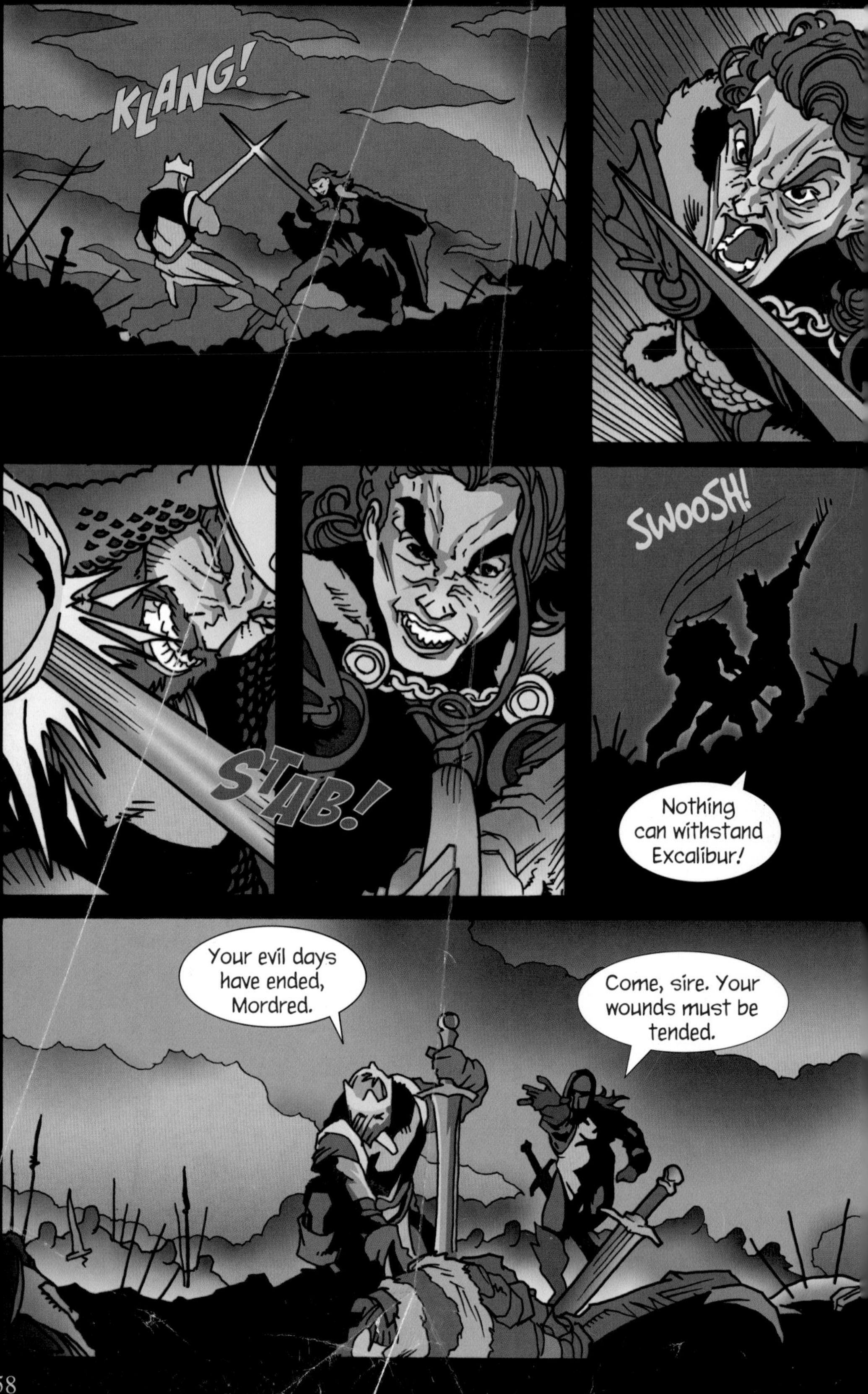
KLANG!
STAB!
SWOOSH!
Nothing can withstand Excalibur!
Your evil days have ended, Mordred.
Come, sire. Your wounds must be tended.

ABOUT SIR THOMAS MALORY

The story of King Arthur is an ancient legend that storytellers passed down for many generations. The story was first told sometime before the 11th century. Finally, in the 15th century, Sir Thomas Malory wrote down his version of these stories. He titled the collection *The Book of King Arthur and His Noble Knights of the Round Table.*

People know little about Malory's interest in the stories of King Arthur. He likely heard different versions of these stories when he was growing up. Perhaps his life experience as a knight helped him better understand the good and evil forces in the King Arthur stories.

ABOUT THE AUTHOR

M. C. Hall has written more than 80 fiction and nonfiction books for children, including science books, biographies, and fairy tales. She likes to read, walk on the beach, garden, and ski. She lives in the Boston area.

ABOUT THE ILLUSTRATOR

C. E. Richards grew up reading comic books, C. S. Lewis, J. R. R. Tolkien, and watching *Star Wars*. He is a graduate of Savannah College of Art and lives in Atlanta, where he is working on book and magazine illustrations, comic books, poster design, playbill illustration, and album artwork for CDs.

GLOSSARY

archbishop (arch-BISH-up)—the ruler of bishops in some Christian religions

duke (DOOK)—in Britain, a person ranked lower than a prince

fortress (FOR-truhss)—a group of buildings protected by walls and forts

hermit (HUR-mit)—a person who lives alone and away from others

joust (JOWST)—a battle with lances or spears fought between knights on horseback

moat (MOHT)—a deep, wide ditch filled with water that surrounds a castle or fortress and keeps people away

perilous (PARE-uhl-uhss)—dangerous

potion (PO-shuhn)—a drink with special powers

prophesy (PROF-uh-see)—a prediction

rebel (REB-uhl)—a person who doesn't follow rules

scabbard (SKAB-urd)—a case that people wear to hold a sword

wizard (WIZ-urd)—a person with magical powers

BACKGROUND ON THE KNIGHTS OF THE ROUND TABLE

The stories of King Arthur and the Knights of the Round Table take place in Britain during the Middle Ages, a time period that lasted from the 5th to the 15th century A.D. This was a period of unrest in Britain and Europe as people fought many wars for control of the land. Britain wasn't a united country at the time.
Kings and lords throughout what is now England, Wales, and Scotland ruled over small regions scattered across the countryside.

Many people wonder if the legends of King Arthur are real and if the places in the story really existed.
Some historians believe that the castle Camelot and the island of Avalon are based on real places in England. For example, some people believe that Arthur is buried beneath the town of Glastonbury. Visitors still travel to England to retrace the steps of King Arthur and his knights.

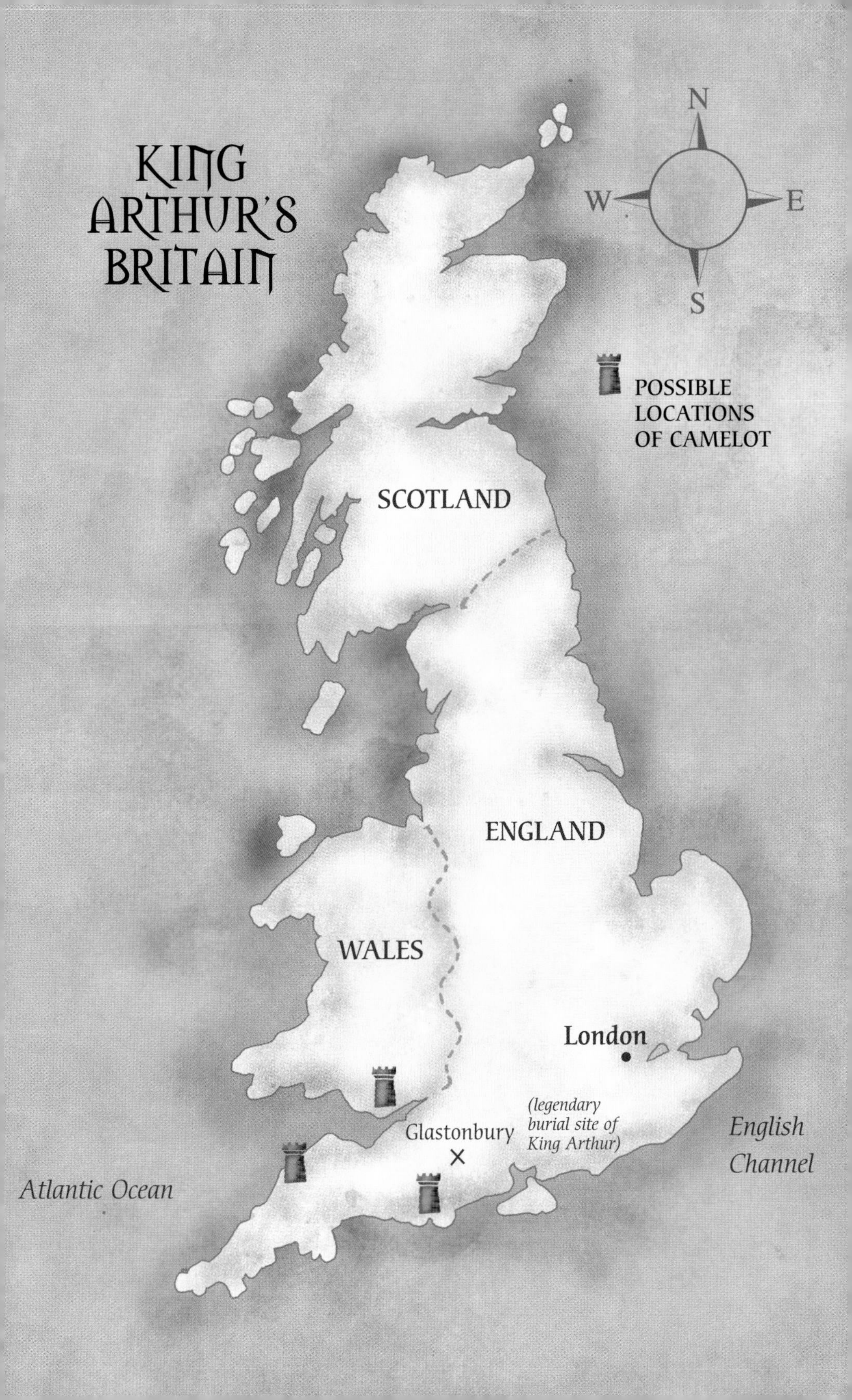
KING ARTHUR'S BRITAIN
N
W
E
S
POSSIBLE LOCATIONS OF CAMELOT
SCOTLAND
ENGLAND
WALES
London
Glastonbury
(legendary burial site of King Arthur)
English Channel
Atlantic Ocean

DISCUSSION QUESTIONS

1. Why did the Round Table break into two pieces?

2. At the end of the story, we find out that King Arthur and the Knights of the Round Table will return someday. Name some times when you could use the help of Arthur and the knights.

3. Would you like to go back to the times of King Arthur? Why or why not?

4. When Arthur was a boy, how did people know that he was really the king?

WRITING PROMPTS

1. Imagine that you were given the sword Excalibur. Explain what you would do with its magical powers. (Remember, the sword can only be used for good.)

2. Describe your favorite character in the story. Is it Arthur or Guinevere? Lancelot or Merlin? What does your favorite character look like? Why do you like this character the best?

3. The Knights of the Round Table go on a quest to find the Holy Grail. Their journey took a long time. Write about a quest, or journey, that you went on. What did you find at the end of it?

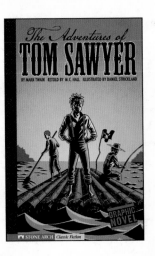

OTHER BOOKS

The Adventures of
TOM SAWYER
BY MARK TWAIN RETOLD BY M. C. HALL ILLUSTRATED BY DANIEL STRICKLAND
GRAPHIC NOVEL
STONE ARCH Classic Fiction

The Adventures of Tom Sawyer

Tom Sawyer is the cleverest of characters, constantly outwitting those around him. Then there is Huckleberry Finn, the envy of the town's schoolchildren because he has the rare gift of complete freedom, never attending school or answering to anyone but himself. After Tom and Huck witness a murder, they find themselves on a series of adventures that lead them to some seriously frightening situations.

THE
HUNCHBACK
OF NOTRE DAME
GRAPHIC NOVEL
STONE ARCH Classic Fiction

The Hunchback of Notre Dame

Hidden away in the bell tower of the Cathedral of Notre Dame, Quasimodo is treated like a beast. Although he is gentle and kind, he has the reputation of a frightening monster because of his physical deformities. He develops affection for Esmeralda, a gypsy girl who shows him kindness in return. When the girl is sentenced to an unfair death by hanging, Quasimodo is determined to save her. But those closest to Quasimodo have other plans for the gypsy.

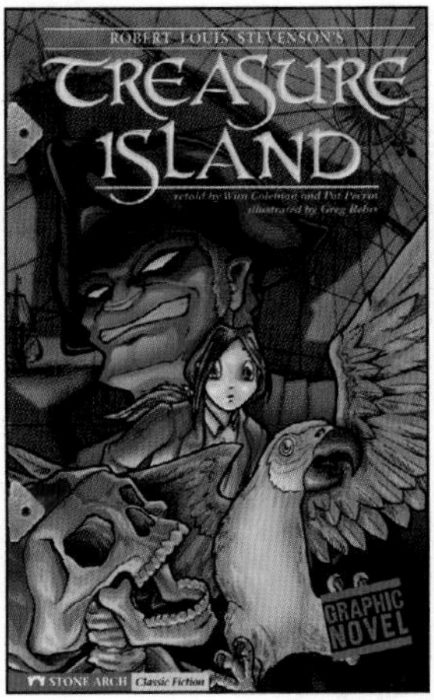
ROBERT LOUIS STEVENSON'S
TREASURE ISLAND
GRAPHIC NOVEL
STONE ARCH Classic Fiction

Treasure Island

Jim Hawkins had no idea what he was getting into when the pirate Billy Bones showed up at the doorstep of his mother's inn. When Billy dies suddenly, Jim is left to unlock his old sea chest, which reveals money, a journal, and a treasure map. Joined by a band of honorable men, Jim sets sail on a dangerous voyage to locate the loot on a faraway island. The violent sea is only one of the dangers they face. They soon encounter a band of bloodthirsty pirates determined to make the treasure their own!

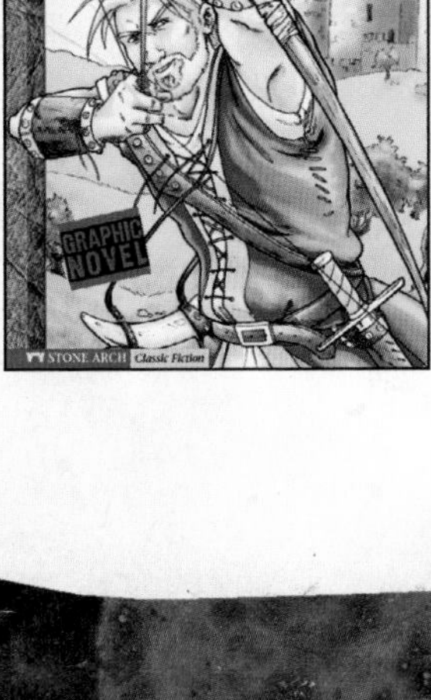
ROBIN HOOD
GRAPHIC NOVEL
STONE ARCH Classic Fiction

Robin Hood

Robin Hood and his Merrie Men are the heroes of Sherwood Forest. Taking from the rich and giving to the poor, Robin Hood and his loyal followers fight for the downtrodden and oppressed. As they outwit the cruel Sheriff of Nottingham, Robin Hood and his Merrie Men are led on a series of exciting adventures.

INTERNET SITES

Do you want to know more about subjects related to this book? Or are you interested in learning about other topics? Then check out FactHound, a fun, easy way to find Internet sites.

Our investigative staff has already sniffed out great sites for you!

Here's how to use FactHound:

1. Visit *www.facthound.com*

2. Select your grade level.

3. To learn more about subjects related to this book, type in the book's ISBN number: **1598890484.**

4. Click the **Fetch It** button.

FactHound will fetch the best Internet sites for you!